The Long Shadow

by
B.M Bower

Other Works
by
B.M Bower

Cabin Fever
Casey Ryan
Chip, of the Flying U
Cow-Country
The Flying U Ranch
The Flying U's Last Stand
Good Indian
The Gringos
The Happy Family
The Heritage of the Sioux
Her Prairie Knight
Jean of the Lazy A
Lonesome Land
The Lonesome Trail and Other Stories
The Long Shadow
The Lookout Man
The Lure of the Dim Trails
The Phantom Herd
The Quirt
The Range Dwellers
Rowdy of the Cross L
Skyrider
Starr, of the Desert
The Thunder Bird
The Trail of the White Mule
The Uphill Climb

CHAPTER I.
Charming Billy Has a Visitor.

The wind, rising again as the sun went down, mourned lonesomely at the northwest corner of the cabin, as if it felt the desolateness of the barren, icy hills and the black hollows between, and of the angry red sky with its purple shadows lowering over the unhappy land—and would make fickle friendship with some human thing. Charming Billy, hearing the crooning wail of it, knew well the portent and sighed. Perhaps he, too, felt something of the desolateness without and perhaps he, too, longed for some human companionship.

He sent a glance of half-conscious disapproval around the untidy cabin. He had been dreaming aimlessly of a place he had seen not so long ago; a place where the stove was black and shining, with a fire crackling cheeringly inside and a teakettle with straight, unmarred spout and dependable handle singing placidly to itself and puffing steam with an air of lazy comfort, as if it were smoking a cigarette. The stove had stood in the southwest corner of the room, and the room was warm with the heat of it; and the floor was white and had a strip of rag carpet reaching from the table to a corner of the stove. There was a red cloth with knotted fringe on the table, and a bed in another corner had a red-and-white patchwork spread and puffy white pillows. There had been a woman—but Charming Billy shut his eyes, mentally, to the woman, because he was not accustomed to them and he was not at all sure that he wanted to be accustomed; they did not fit in with the life he lived. He felt dimly that, in a way, they were like the heaven his mother had taught him—altogether perfect and altogether unattainable and not to be thought of with any degree of familiarity. So his memory of the woman was indistinct, as of something which did not properly belong to the picture. He clung instead to the memory of the warm stove, and the strip of carpet, and the table with the red cloth, and to the puffy, white pillows on the bed.

The wind mourned again insistently at the corner. Billy lifted his head and looked once more around the cabin. The reality was depressing—doubly depressing in contrast to the memory of that other room. A stove stood in the southwest corner, but it was not black and shining; it was rust-red and ash-littered, and the ashes had overflowed the hearth and spilled to the unswept floor. A dented lard-pail without a handle did meagre duty as a teakettle, and balanced upon a corner of the stove was a dirty frying pan. The fire had gone dead and the room was chill with the rising of the wind. The table was filled with empty cans and tin plates and cracked, oven-stained bowls and iron-handled knives and forks, and the bunk in the corner was a tumble of gray blankets and unpleasant, red-flowered comforts—corner-wads, Charming Billy was used to calling them—and for pillows there were two square, calico-covered cushions, depressingly ugly in pattern and not over-clean.

Billy sighed again, threaded a needle with coarse, black thread and attacked petulantly a long rent in his coat.

"Darn this bushwhacking all over God's earth after a horse a man can't stay with, nor even hold by the bridle reins," he complained dispiritedly. "I could uh cleaned the blamed shack up so it would look like folks was living here—and I woulda, if I didn't have to set all day and toggle up the places in my clothes"—Billy muttered incoherently over a knot in his thread. "I've been plumb puzzled, all winter, to know whether it's man or cattle I'm supposed to chappyrone. If it's man, this coat has sure got the marks uh the trade, all right." He drew the needle spitefully through the cloth.

The wind gathered breath and swooped down upon the cabin so that Billy felt the jar of it. "I don't see what's got the matter of the weather," he grumbled. "Yuh just get a chinook that starts water running down the coulées, and then the wind switches and she freezes up solid—and that means tailing-up poor cows and calves by the dozen—and for your side-partner yuh get dealt out to yuh a pilgrim that don't know nothing and can't ride a wagon seat, hardly, and that's bound to keep a *dawg*! And the Old Man stands for that kind uh thing and has forbid accidents happening to it—oh, hell!"

This last was inspired by a wriggling movement under the bunk. A black dog, of the apologetic drooping sort that always has its tail sagging and matted with burrs, crawled out and sidled past Billy with a deprecating wag or two when he caught his unfriendly glance, and shambled over to the door that he might sniff suspiciously the cold air coming in through the crack beneath.

Billy eyed him malevolently. "A dog in a line-camp is a plumb disgrace! I don't see why the Old Man stands for it—or the Pilgrim, either; it's a toss-up which is the worst. Yuh smell him coming, do yuh?" he snarled. "It's about *time* he was coming—me here eating dried apricots and tapioca steady diet (nobody but a pilgrim would fetch tapioca into a line-camp, and if he does it again you'll sure be missing the only friend yuh got) and him gone four days when he'd oughta been back the second. Get out and welcome him, darn yuh!" He gathered the coat under one arm that he might open the door, and hurried the dog outside with a threatening boot toe. The wind whipped his brown cheeks so that he closed the door hastily and retired to the cheerless shelter of the cabin.

"Another blizzard coming, if I know the signs. And if the Pilgrim don't show up to-night with the grub and tobacco—But I reckon the dawg smelt him coming, all right." He fingered uncertainly a very flabby tobacco sack, grew suddenly reckless and made himself an exceedingly thin cigarette with the remaining crumbs of tobacco and what little he could glean from the pockets of the coat he was mending. Surely, the Pilgrim would remember his tobacco! Incapable as he was, he could scarcely forget that, after the extreme emphasis Charming Billy had laid upon the getting, and the penalties attached to its oversight.

Outside, the dog was barking spasmodically; but Billy, being a product of the cattle industry pure and simple, knew not the way of dogs. He took it for granted that the

Pilgrim was arriving with the grub, though he was too disgusted with his delay to go out and make sure. Dogs always barked at everything impartially—when they were not gnawing surreptitiously at bones or snooping in corners for scraps, or planting themselves deliberately upon your clothes. Even when the noise subsided to throaty growls he failed to recognize the symptoms; he was taking long, rapturous mouthfuls of smoke and gazing dreamily at his coat, for it was his first cigarette since yesterday.

When some one rapped lightly he jumped, although he was not a man who owned unsteady nerves. It was very unusual, that light tapping. When any one wanted to come in he always opened the door without further ceremony. Still, there was no telling what strange freak might impel the Pilgrim—he who insisted on keeping a dog in a line-camp!—so Billy recovered himself and called out impatiently: "Aw, come on in! Don't be a plumb fool," and never moved from his place.

The door opened queerly; slowly, and with a timidity not at all in keeping with the blundering assertiveness of the Pilgrim. When a young woman showed for a moment against the bleak twilight and then stepped inside, Charming Billy caught at the table for support, and the coat he was holding dropped to the floor. He did not say a word: he just stared.

The girl closed the door behind her with something of defiance, that did not in the least impose upon one. "Good evening," she said briskly, though even in his chaotic state of mind Billy felt the tremble in her voice. "It's rather late for making calls, but—" She stopped and caught her breath nervously, as if she found it impossible to go on being brisk and at ease. "I was riding, and my horse slipped and hurt himself so he couldn't walk, and I saw this cabin from up on the hill over there. So I came here, because it was so far home—and I thought—maybe—" She looked with big, appealing brown eyes at Billy, who felt himself a brute without in the least knowing why. "I'm Flora Bridger; you know, my father has taken up a ranch over on Shell Creek, and—"

"I'm very glad to meet you," said Charming Billy stammeringly. "Won't you sit down? I—I wish I'd known company was coming." He smiled reassuringly, and then glanced frowningly around the cabin. Even for a line-camp, he told himself disgustedly, it was "pretty sousy." "You must be cold," he added, seeing her glance toward the stove. "I'll have a fire going right away; I've been pretty busy and just let things slide." He threw the un-smoked half of his cigarette into the ashes and felt not a quiver of regret. He knew who she was, now; she was the daughter he had heard about, and who belonged to the place where the stove was black and shining and the table had a red cloth with knotted fringe. It must have been her mother whom he had seen there—but she had looked very young to be mother of a young lady.

Charming Billy brought himself rigidly to consider the duties of a host; swept his arm across a bench to clear it of sundry man garments, and asked her again to sit down.

When she did so, he saw that her fingers were clasped tightly to hold her from shivering, and he raved inwardly at his shiftlessness the while he hurried to light a fire in the stove.

"Too bad your horse fell," he remarked stupidly, gathering up the handful of shavings he had whittled from a piece of pine board. "I always hate to see a horse get hurt." It was not what he had wanted to say, but he could not seem to put just the right thing into words. What he wanted was to make her feel that there was nothing out of the ordinary in her being there, and that he was helpful and sympathetic without being in the least surprised. In all his life on the range he had never had a young woman walk into a line-camp at dusk—a strange young woman who tried pitifully to be at ease and whose eyes gave the lie to her manner—and he groped confusedly for just the right way in which to meet the situation.

"I know your father," he said, fanning a tiny blaze among the shavings with his hat, which had been on his head until he remembered and removed it in deference to her presence. "But I ain't a very good neighbor, I guess; I never seem to have time to be sociable. It's lucky your horse fell close enough so yuh could walk in to camp; I've had that happen to me more than once, and it ain't never pleasant—but it's worse when there ain't any camp to walk to. I've had that happen, too."

The fire was snapping by then, and manlike he swept the ashes to the floor. The girl watched him, politely disapproving. "I don't want to be a trouble," she said, with less of constraint; for Charming Billy, whether he knew it or not, had reassured her immensely. "I know men hate to cook, so when I get warm, and the water is hot, I'll cook supper for you," she offered. "And then I won't mind having you help me to get home."

"I guess it won't be any trouble—but I don't mind cooking. You—you better set still and rest," murmured Charming Billy, quite red. Of course, she would want supper—and there were dried apricots, and a very little tapioca! He felt viciously that he could kill the Pilgrim and be glad. The Pilgrim was already two days late with the supplies he had been sent after because he was not to be trusted with the duties pertaining to a line-camp—and Billy had not the wide charity that could conjure excuses for the delinquent.

"I'll let you wash the dishes," promised Miss Bridger generously. "But I'll cook the supper—really, I want to, you know. I won't say I'm not hungry, because I am. This Western air does give one *such* an appetite, doesn't it? And then I walked miles, it seems to me; so that ought to be an excuse, oughtn't it? Now, if you'll show me where the coffee is—"

She had risen and was looking at him expectantly, with a half smile that seemed to invite one to comradeship. Charming Billy looked at her helplessly, and turned a shade less brown.

"The—there isn't any," he stammered guiltily. "The Pilgrim—I mean Walland—Fred Walland—"

"It doesn't matter in the least," Miss Bridger assured him hastily. "One can't keep everything in the house all the time, so far from any town. We're often out of things, at home. Last week, only, I upset the vanilla bottle, and then we were completely out of vanilla till just yesterday." She smiled again confidingly, and Billy tried to seem very sympathetic—though of a truth, to be out of vanilla did not at that moment seem to him a serious catastrophe. "And really, I like tea better, you know. I only said coffee because father told me cowboys drink it a great deal. Tea is so much quicker and easier to make."

Billy dug his nails into his palms. "There—Miss Bridger," he blurted desperately, "I've got to tell yuh—there isn't a thing in the shack except some dried apricots—and maybe a spoonful or two of tapioca. The Pilgrim—" He stopped to search his brain for words applicable to the Pilgrim and still mild enough for the ears of a lady.

"Well, never mind. We can rough it—it will be lots of fun!" the girl laughed so readily as almost to deceive Billy, standing there in his misery. That a woman should come to him for help, and he not even able to give her food, was almost unbearable. It were well for the Pilgrim that Charming Billy Boyle could not at that moment lay hands upon him.

"It will be fun," she laughed again in his face. "If the—the grubstake is down to a whisper (that's the way you say it, isn't it?) there will be all the more credit coming to the cook when you see all the things she can do with dried apricots and tapioca. May I rummage?"

"Sure," assented Billy, dazedly moving aside so that she might reach the corner where three boxes were nailed by their bottoms to the wall, curtained with gayly flowered calico and used for a cupboard. "The Pilgrim," he began for the third time to explain, "went after grub and is taking his time about getting back. He'd oughta been here day before yesterday. We might eat his dawg," he suggested, gathering spirit now that her back was toward him.

Her face appeared at one side of the calico curtain. "I know something better than eating the dog," she announced triumphantly. "Down there in the willows where I crossed the creek—I came down that low, saggy place in the hill—I saw a lot of chickens or something—partridges, maybe you call them—roosting in a tree with their feathers all puffed out. It's nearly dark, but they're worth trying for, don't you think? That is, if you have a gun," she added, as if she had begun to realize how meagre were his possessions. "If you don't happen to have one, we can do all right with what there is here, you know."

Billy flushed a little, and for answer took down his gun and belt from where they hung upon the wall, buckled the belt around his slim middle and picked up his hat. "If they're there yet, I'll get some, sure," he promised. "You just keep the fire going till I come back, and I'll wash the dishes. Here, I'll shut the dawg in the house; he's always plumb crazy with ambition to do just what yuh don't want him to do, and I don't want him following." He smiled upon her again (he was finding that rather easy to do) and closed the door lingeringly behind him. Having never tried to analyze his feelings, he did not wonder why he stepped so softly along the frozen path that led to the stable, or why he felt that glow of elation which comes to a man only when he has found something precious in his sight.

"I wish I hadn't eat the last uh the flour this morning," he regretted anxiously. "I coulda made some bread; there's a little yeast powder left in the can. Darn the Pilgrim!"

CHAPTER II.
Prune Pie and Coon-can.

Of a truth, Charming Billy Boyle, living his life in the wide land that is too big and too far removed from the man-made world for any but the strong of heart, knew little indeed of women—her kind of women. When he returned with two chickens and found that the floor had been swept so thoroughly as to look strange to him, and that all his scattered belongings were laid in a neat pile upon the foot of the bunk which was unfamiliar under straightened blankets and pitifully plumped pillows, he was filled with astonishment. Miss Bridger smiled a little and went on washing the dishes.

"It's beginning to storm, isn't it?" she remarked. "But we'll eat chicken stew before we—before I start home. If you have a horse that I can borrow till morning, father will bring it back."

Billy scattered a handful of feathers on the floor and gained a little time by stooping to pick them up one by one. "I've been wondering about that," he said reluctantly. "It's just my luck not to have a gentle hoss in camp. I've got two, but they ain't safe for women. The Pilgrim's got one hoss that might uh done if it was here, which it ain't."

She looked disturbed, though she tried to hide it. "I can ride pretty well," she ventured.

Without glancing at her, Charming Billy shook his head. "You're all right here"—he stopped to pick up more feathers—"and it wouldn't be safe for yuh to try it. One hoss is mean about mounting; yuh couldn't get within a rod of him. The other one is a holy terror to pitch when anything strange gets near him. I wouldn't let yuh try it." Charming Billy was sorry—that showed in his voice—but he was also firm.

Miss Bridger thoughtfully wiped a tin spoon. Billy gave her a furtive look and dropped his head at the way the brightness had gone out of her face. "They'll be worried, at home," she said quietly.

"A little worry beats a funeral," Billy retorted sententiously, instinctively mastering the situation because she was a woman and he must take care of her. "I reckon I could—" He stopped abruptly and plucked savagely at a stubborn wing feather.

"Of course! You could ride over and bring back a horse!" She caught eagerly at his half-spoken offer. "It's a lot of bother for you, but I—I'll be very much obliged." Her face was bright again.

"You'd be alone here—"

"I'm not the least bit afraid to stay alone. I wouldn't mind that at all."

Billy hesitated, met a look in her eyes that he did not like to see there, and yielded. Obviously, from her viewpoint that was the only thing to do. A cowpuncher who has ridden the range since he was sixteen should not shirk a night ride in a blizzard, or fear losing the trail. It was not storming so hard a man might not ride ten miles—that is, a man like Charming Billy Boyle.

After that he was in great haste to be gone, and would scarcely wait until Miss Bridger, proudly occupying the position of cook, told him that the chicken stew was ready. Indeed, he would have gone without eating it if she had not protested in a way that made Billy foolishly glad to submit; as it was, he saddled his horse while he waited, and reached for his sheepskin-lined, "sour-dough" coat before the last mouthful was fairly swallowed. At the last minute he unbuckled his gun belt and held it out to her.

"I'll leave you this," he remarked, with an awkward attempt to appear careless. "You'll feel safer if you have a gun, and—and if you're scared at anything, shoot it." He finished with another smile that lighted wonderfully his face and his eyes.

She shook her head. "I've often stayed alone. There's nothing in the world to be afraid of—and anyway, I'll have the dog. Thank you, all the same."

Charming Billy looked at her, opened his mouth and closed it without speaking. He laid the gun down on the table and turned to go. "If anything scares yuh," he repeated stubbornly, "shoot it. Yuh don't want to count too much on that dawg."

He discovered then that Flora Bridger was an exceedingly willful young woman. She picked up the gun, overtook him, and fairly forced it into his hands. "Don't be silly; I don't want it. I'm not such a coward as all that. You must have a very poor opinion of women. I—I'm deadly afraid of a gun!"

Billy was not particularly impressed by the last statement, but he felt himself at the end of his resources and buckled the belt around him without more argument. After all, he told himself, it was not likely that she would have cause for alarm in the few hours that he would be gone, and those hours he meant to trim down as much as possible.

Out of the coulée where the high wall broke the force of the storm, he faced the snow and wind and pushed on doggedly. It was bitter riding, that night, but he had seen worse and the discomfort of it troubled him little; it was not the first time he had bent head to snow and driving wind and had kept on so for hours. What harassed him most were the icy hills where the chinook had melted the snow, and the north wind, sweeping over, had frozen it all solid again. He could not ride as fast as he had counted upon riding, and he realized that it would be long hours before he could get back to the cabin with a horse from Bridger's.

Billy could not tell when first came the impulse to turn back. It might have been while he was working his way cautiously up a slippery coulée side, or it might have come suddenly just when he stopped; for stop he did (just when he should logically have ridden faster because the way was smoother) and turned his horse's head downhill.

"If she'd kept the gun—" he muttered, apologizing to himself for the impulse, and flayed his horse with his *romal* because he did not quite understand himself and so was ill at ease. Afterward, when he was loping steadily down the coulée bottom with his fresh-made tracks pointing the way before him, he broke out irrelevantly and viciously: "A real, old range rider yuh can bank on, one way or the other—but damn a pilgrim!"

The wind and the snow troubled him not so much now that his face was not turned to meet them, but it seemed to him that the way was rougher and that the icy spots were more dangerous to the bones of himself and his horse than when he had come that way before. He did not know why he need rage at the pace he must at times keep, and it did strike him as being a foolish thing to do— this turning back when he was almost halfway to his destination; but for every time he thought that, he urged his horse more.

The light from the cabin window, twinkling through the storm, cheered him a little, which was quite as unreasonable as his uneasiness. It did not, however, cause him to linger at turning his horse into the stable and shutting the door upon him. When he passed the cabin window he glanced anxiously in and saw dimly through the half-frosted glass that Miss Bridger was sitting against the wall by the table, tight-lipped and watchful. He hurried to the door and pushed it open.

"Why, hello," greeted the Pilgrim uncertainly, The Pilgrim was standing in the centre of the room, and he did not look particularly pleased. Charming Billy, every nerve on edge, took in the situation at a glance, kicked the Pilgrim's dog and shook the snow from his hat.

"I lost the trail," he lied briefly and went over to the stove. He did not look at Miss Bridger directly, but he heard the deep breath which she took.

"Well, so did I," the Pilgrim began eagerly, with just the least slurring of his syllables. "I'd have been here before dark, only one of the horses slipped and lamed himself. It was much as ever I got home at all. He come in on three legs, and toward the last them three like to went back on him."

"Which hoss?" asked Billy, though he felt pessimistically that he knew without being told. The Pilgrim's answer confirmed his pessimism. Of course, it was the only gentle horse they had.

"Say, Billy, I forgot your tobacco," drawled the Pilgrim, after a very short silence which Billy used for much rapid thinking.

Ordinarily, Billy would have considered the over sight as something of a catastrophe, but he passed it up as an unpleasant detail and turned to the girl. "It's storming something fierce," he told her in an exceedingly matter-of-fact way, "but I think it'll let up by daylight so we can tackle it. Right now it's out of the question; so we'll have another supper—a regular blowout this time, with coffee and biscuits and all those luxuries. How are yuh on making biscuits?"

So he got her out of the corner, where she had looked too much at bay to please him, and in making the biscuits she lost the watchful look from her eyes. But she was not the Flora Bridger who had laughed at their makeshifts and helped cook the chicken, and Charming Billy, raving inwardly at the change, in his heart damned fervently the Pilgrim.

In the hours that followed, Billy showed the stuff he was made of. He insisted upon cooking the things that would take the longest time to prepare; boasted volubly of the prune pies he could make, and then set about demonstrating his skill and did not hurry the prunes in the stewing. He fished out a package of dried lima beans and cooked some of them, changing the water three times and always adding cold water. For all that, supper was eventually ready and eaten and the dishes washed—with Miss Bridger wiping them and with the Pilgrim eying them both in a way that set on edge the teeth of Charming Billy. When there was absolutely nothing more to keep them busy, Billy got the cards and asked Miss Bridger if she could play coon-can—which was the only game he knew that was rigidly "two-handed." She did not know the game and he insisted upon teaching her, though the Pilgrim glowered and hinted strongly at seven-up or something else which they could all play.

"I don't care for seven-up," Miss Bridger quelled, speaking to him for the first time since Billy returned. "I want to learn this game that—er—Billy knows." There was a slight hesitation on the name, which was the only one she knew to call him by.

The Pilgrim grunted and retired to the stove, rattled the lids ill-naturedly and smoked a vile cigar which he had brought from town. After that he sat and glowered at the two.

Billy did the best he could to make the time pass quickly. He had managed to seat Miss Bridger so that her back was toward the stove and the Pilgrim, and he did it so unobtrusively that neither guessed his reason. He taught her coon-can, two-handed whist and Chinese solitaire before a gray lightening outside proclaimed that the night was over. Miss Bridger, heavy-eyed and languid, turned her face to the window; Billy swept the cards together and stacked them with an air of finality.

"I guess we can hit the trail now without losing ourselves," he remarked briskly. "Pilgrim, come on out and help me saddle up; we'll see if that old skate of yours is able to travel."

The Pilgrim got up sullenly and went out, and Billy followed him silently. His own horse had stood with the saddle on all night, and the Pilgrim snorted when he saw it. But Billy only waited till the Pilgrim had put his saddle on the gentlest mount they had, then took the reins from him and led both horses to the door.

"All right," he called to the girl; helped her into the saddle and started off, with not a word of farewell from Miss Bridger to the Pilgrim.

The storm had passed and the air was still and biting cold. The eastern sky was stained red and purple with the rising sun, and beneath the feet of their horses the snow creaked frostily. So they rode down the coulée and then up a long slope to the top, struck the trail and headed straight north with a low line of hills for their goal. And in the hour and a half of riding, neither spoke a dozen words.

At the door of her own home Billy left her, and gathered up the reins of the Pilgrim's horse. "Well, good-by. Oh,

had been so anxious to get her away from under the man's leering gaze that he had not thought of eating. And if the Pilgrim had been a *man*, he might have sent him over to Bridger's for her father and a horse. But the Pilgrim would have lost himself, or have refused to go, and the latter possibility would have caused a scene unfit for the eyes of a young woman.

So he rode slowly and thought of many things he might have done which would have been better than what he did do; and wondered what the girl thought about it and if she blamed him for not doing something different. And for every mile of the way he cursed the Pilgrim anew.

In that unfriendly mood he opened the door of the cabin, stood a minute just inside, then closed it after him with a slam. The cabin, in contrast with the bright light of sun shining on new-fallen snow, was dark and so utterly cheerless and chill that he shrugged shoulders impatiently at its atmosphere, which was as intangibly offensive as had been the conduct of the Pilgrim.

The Pilgrim was sprawled upon the bunk with his face in his arms, snoring in a peculiarly rasping way that Billy, heavy-eyed as he was, resented most unreasonably. Also, the untidy table showed that the Pilgrim had eaten unstintedly—and Billy was exceedingly hungry. He went over and lifted a snowy boot to the ribs of the sleeper and commanded him bluntly to "Come alive."

"What-yuh-want?" mumbled the Pilgrim thickly, making one word of the three and lifting his red-rimmed eyes to the other. He raised to an elbow with a lazy doubling of his body and stared dully for a space before he grinned unpleasantly. "Took 'er home all right, did yuh?" he leered, as if they two were in possession of a huge joke of the kind which may not be told in mixed company.

If Charming Billy Boyle had needed anything more to stir him to the fighting point, that one sentence admirably supplied the lack. "Yuh low-down skunk!" he cried, and struck him full upon the insulting, smiling mouth. "If I was as rotten-minded as you are, I'd go drown myself in the stalest alkali hole I could find. I dunno why I'm dirtying my hands on yuh—yuh ain't fit to be clubbed to death with a tent pole!" He was, however, using his hands freely and to very good purpose, probably feeling that, since the Pilgrim was much bigger than he, there was need of getting a good start.

But the Pilgrim was not the sort to lie on his bunk and take a thrashing. He came up after the second blow, pushing Billy back with the very weight of his body, and they were fighting all over the little cabin, surging against the walls and the table and knocking the coffee-pot off the stove as they lurched this way and that. Not much was said after the first outburst of Billy's, save a panting curse now and then between blows, a threat gasped while they wrestled.

It was the dog, sneaking panther-like behind Billy and setting treacherous teeth viciously into his leathern chaps, that brought the crisis. Billy tore loose and snatched his gun from the scabbard at his hip, held the Pilgrim momentarily at bay with one hand while he took a shot at the dog, missed, kicked him back from another rush, and turned again on the Pilgrim.

"Get that dawg outdoors, then," he panted, "or I'll kill him sure." The Pilgrim, for answer, struck a blow that staggered Billy, and tried to grab the gun. Billy, hooking a foot around a table-leg, threw it between them, swept the blood from his eyes and turned his gun once more on the dog that was watching treacherously for another chance.

"That's the time I got him," he gritted through the smoke, holding the Pilgrim quiet before him with the gun. "But I've got a heap more respect for him than I have for you, yuh damn', low-down brute. I'd ought to kill yuh like I would a coyote. Yuh throw your traps together and light out uh here, before I forget and shoot yuh up. There ain't room in this camp for you and me no more."

The Pilgrim backed, eying Billy malevolently. "I never done nothing," he defended sullenly. "The boss'll have something to say about this—and I'll kill you first chance I get, for shooting my dog."

"It ain't what yuh done, it's what yuh woulda done if you'd had the chance," answered Billy, for the first time finding words for what was surging bitterly in the heart of him. "And I'm willing to take a whirl with yuh any old time; any dawg that'll lick the boots of a man like you had ought to be shot for not having more sense. I ain't saying anything about him biting me—which I'd kill him for, anyhow. Now, git! I want my breakfast, and I can't eat with any relish whilst you're spoiling the air in here for me."

At heart the Pilgrim was a coward as well as a beast, and he packed his few belongings hurriedly and started for the door.

"Come back here, and drag your dawg outside," commanded Billy, and the Pilgrim obeyed.

"You'll hear about this later on," he snarled. "The boss won't stand for anything like this. I never done a thing, and I'm going to tell him so."

"Aw, go on and tell him, yuh—!" snapped Billy. "Only yuh don't want to get absent-minded enough to come back— not whilst I'm here; things unpleasant might happen." He stood in the doorway and watched while the Pilgrim saddled his horse and rode away. When not even the pluckety-pluck of his horse's feet came back to offend the ears of him, Charming Billy put away his gun and went in and hoisted the overturned table upon its legs again. A coarse, earthenware plate, which the Pilgrim had used for his breakfast, lay unbroken at the feet of him. Billy picked it up, went to the door and cast it violently forth, watching with grim satisfaction the pieces when they scattered over the frozen ground. "No white man'll ever have to eat after *him*," he muttered. To ease his outraged feelings still farther, he picked up the Pilgrim's knife and fork, and sent them after the plate—and knives and forks were not numerous in that particular camp, either. After that he felt better and picked up the coffee-pot, lighted a fire and cooked himself some breakfast, which he ate hungrily, his wrath cooling a bit with the cheer of warm food and strong coffee.

The routine work of the line-camp was performed in a hurried, perfunctory manner that day. Charming Billy, riding the high-lines to make sure the cattle had not drifted where they should not, was vaguely ill at ease. He told himself it was the want of a smoke that made him uncomfortable, and he planned a hurried trip to Hardup, if the weather held good for another day, when he would lay in a supply of tobacco and papers that would last till roundup. This running out every two or three weeks, and living in hell till you got more, was plumb wearisome and unnecessary.

On the way back, his trail crossed that of a breed wolfer on his way into the Bad Lands. Billy immediately asked for tobacco, and the breed somewhat reluctantly opened his pack and exchanged two small sacks for a two-bit piece. Billy, rolling a cigarette with eager fingers, felt for the moment a deep satisfaction with life. He even felt some compunction about killing the Pilgrim's dog, when he passed the body stiffening on the snow. "Poor devil! Yuh hadn't ought to expect much from a dawg—and he was a heap more white-acting than what his owner was," was his tribute to the dead.

It seemed as though, when he closed the cabin door behind him, he somehow shut out his newborn satisfaction. "A shack with one window is sure unpleasant when the sun is shining outside," he said fretfully to himself. "This joint looks a heap like a cellar. I wonder what the girl thought of it; I reckon it looked pretty sousy, to her—and them with everything shining. Oh, hell!" He took off his chaps and his spurs, rolled another cigarette and smoked it meditatively. When it had burned down so that it came near scorching his lips, he lighted a fire, carried water from the creek, filled the dishpan and set it on the stove to heat. "Darn a dirty shack!" he muttered, half apologetically, while he was taking the accumulation of ashes out of the hearth.

For the rest of that day he was exceedingly busy, and he did not attempt further explanations to himself. He overhauled the bunk and spread the blankets out on the wild rose bushes to sun while he cleaned the floor. Billy's way of cleaning the floor was characteristic of the man, and calculated to be effectual in the main without descending to petty details. All superfluous objects that were small enough, he merely pushed as far as possible under the bunk. Boxes and benches he piled on top; then he brought buckets of water and sloshed it upon the worst places, sweeping and spreading it with a broom. When the water grew quite black, he opened the door, swept it outside and sloshed fresh water upon the grimy boards. While he worked, his mind swung slowly back to normal, so that he sang crooningly in an undertone; and the song was what he had sung for months and years, until it was a part of him and had earned him his nickname.

"Oh, where have you been, Billy boy, Billy boy?
Oh, where have you been, charming Billy?
I've been to see my wife,
She's the joy of my life,
She's a young thing and cannot leave her mother."

Certainly it was neither musical nor inspiring, but Billy had somehow adopted the ditty and made it his own, so far as eternally singing it could do so, and his comrades had found it not unpleasant; for the voice of Billy was youthful, and had a melodious smoothness that atoned for much in the way of imbecile words and monotonous tune.

He had washed all the dishes and had repeated the ditty fifteen times, and was for the sixteenth time tunefully inquiring:

Can she make a punkin pie, charming Billy?

when he opened the door to throw out the dishwater, and narrowly escaped landing it full upon the fur-coated form of his foreman.

CHAPTER IV.
Canned.

The foreman came in, blinking at the sudden change from bright light to half twilight, and Charming Billy took the opportunity to kick a sardine can of stove-blacking under the stove where it would not be seen. Some predecessor with domestic instincts had left behind him half a package of "Rising Sun," and Billy had found it and was intending to blacken the stove just as soon as he finished the dishes. That he had left it as a crowning embellishment, rather than making it the foundation of his house-cleaning, only proved his inexperience in that line. Billy had "bached" a great deal, but he had never blacked a stove in his life.

The foreman passed gloved fingers over his eyes, held them there a moment, took them away and gazed in amazement; since he had been foreman of the Double-Crank—and the years were many—Charming Billy Boyle had been one of its "top-hands," and he had never before caught him in the throes of "digging out."

"Fundamental furies!" swore he, in the unorthodox way he had. "Looks like the Pilgrim was right—there's a lady took charge here."

Charming Billy turned red with embarrassment, and then quite pale with rage. "The Pilgrim lied!" he denied sweepingly.

The foreman picked his way over the wet floor, in deference to its comparative cleanliness stepping long so that he might leave as few disfiguring tracks as possible, and unbuttoned his fur coat before the heat of the stove.

"Well, maybe he did," he assented generously, gleaning a box from the pile on the bunk and sitting down, "but it sure looks like corroborative evidence, in here. How about it, Bill?"

"How about what?" countered Billy, his teeth close together.

"The girl, and the dawg, and the fight—but more especially the girl. The Pilgrim—"

"*Damn* the Pilgrim! I wisht I'd a-killed the lying —— The girl's a lady, and he ain't fit to speak her name. She come here last night because her hoss fell and got crippled, and there wasn't a hoss I'd trust at night with her, it was storming so hard, and slippery—and at daylight I put her on the gentlest one we had, and took her home. That's all there is to it. There's nothing to gabble about, and if the Pilgrim goes around shooting off his face—" Billy clicked his teeth ominously.

"Well, that ain't *just* the way he told it," commented the foreman, stooping to expectorate into the hearth and stopping to regard surprisedly its unwonted emptiness. "He said—"

"I don't give a damn what he said," snapped Billy. "He lied, the low-down cur."

"Uh-huh—he said something about you shooting that dawg of his. I saw the carcass out there in the snow." The foreman spoke with careful neutrality.

"I did. I wisht now I'd laid the two of 'em out together. The dawg tried to feed offa my leg. I shot the blame thing." Charming Billy sat down upon the edge of the table—sliding the dishpan out of his way—and folded his arms, and pushed his hat farther back from his forehead. His whole attitude spoke impenitent scorn.

"I also licked the Pilgrim and hazed him away from camp and told him particular not to come back," he informed the other defiantly. He did not add, "What are you going to do about it?" but his tone carried unmistakably that sentiment.

"And the Pilgrim happens to be a stepbrother uh the widow the Old Man is at present running after, and aiming to marry. I was sent over here to put the can onto you, Billy. I hate like thunder to do it, but—" The foreman waved a hand to signify his utter helplessness.

The face of Billy stiffened perceptibly; otherwise he moved not a muscle.

"The Old Man says for you to stay till he can put another man down here in your place, though. He'll send Jim Bleeker soon as he comes back from town—which ain't apt to be for two or three days unless they're short on booze."

Billy caught his breath, hesitated, and reached for his smoking material. It was not till he had licked his cigarette into shape and was feeling in his pocket for a match that he spoke. "I've drawed wages from the Double-Crank for quite a spell, and I always aimed to act white with the outfit. It's more than they're doing by me, but—I'll stay till

Billy grinned a little and went after his bedding, brought it and threw it with a fine disregard for order upon the accumulation of boxes and benches in the bunk. "I'll go feed the hosses, and then I'll cook yuh some supper," he told the foreman still humped comfortably before the stove with his fur coat thrown open to the heat and his spurred boots hoisted upon the hearth. "Better make up your mind to stay till morning; it's getting mighty chilly, outside."

The foreman, at the critical stage of cigarette lighting, grunted unintelligibly. Billy was just laying hand to the door-knob when the foreman looked toward him in the manner of one about to speak. Billy stood and waited inquiringly.

"Say, Bill," drawled Jawbreaker, "yuh never told me her name, yet."

The brows of Charming Billy pinched involuntarily together. "I thought the Pilgrim had wised yuh up to all the details," he said coldly.

"The Pilgrim didn't know; he says yuh never introduced him. And seeing it's serious enough to start yuh on the godly trail uh cleanliness, I'm naturally taking a friendly interest in her, and—"

"Aw—go to hell!" snapped Charming Billy, and went out and slammed the door behind him so that the cabin shook.

CHAPTER V.
The Man From Michigan.

"How old is she, Billy boy, Billy boy,
How old is she, charming Billy?
Twice six, twice seven,
Forty-nine and eleven—
She's a young thing, and cannot leave her mother."

"C'm-awn, yuh lazy old skate! Think I want to sleep out to-night, when town's so clost?" Charming Billy yanked his pack-pony awake and into a shuffling trot over the trail, resettled his hat on his head, sagged his shoulders again and went back to crooning his ditty.

"Can she make a punkin pie, Billy boy, Billy boy,
Can she make a punkin pie, charming Billy?
She can make a punkin pie
Quick's a cat can wink her eye—"

Out ahead, where the trail wound aimlessly around a low sand ridge flecked with scrubby sage half buried in gray snowbanks, a horse whinnied inquiringly; Barney, his own red-roan, perked his ears toward the sound and sent shrill answer. In that land and at that season travelers were never so numerous as to be met with indifference, and Billy felt a slight thrill of expectation. All day—or as much of it as was left after his late sleeping and later breakfast—he had ridden without meeting a soul; now he unconsciously pressed lightly with his spurs to meet the comer.

Around the first bend they went, and the trail was blank before them. "Thought it sounded close," Billy muttered, "but with the wind where it is and the air like this, sound travels farther. I wonder—"

Past the point before them poked a black head, followed slowly by a shambling horse whose dragging hoofs proclaimed his weariness and utter lack of ambition. The rider, Billy decided after one sharp glance, he had never seen before in his life—and nothing lost by it, either, he finished mentally when he came closer.

If the riders had not willed it so the horses would mutually have agreed to stop when they met; that being the way of range horses after carrying speech-hungry men for a season or two. If men meet out there in the land of far horizons and do not stop for a word or two, it is generally because there is bad feeling between them; and horses learn quickly the ways of their masters.

"Hello," greeted Billy tentatively, eying the other measuringly because he was a stranger. "Pretty soft going, ain't it?" He referred to the half-thawed trail.

"Ye-es," hesitated the other, glancing diffidently down at the trail and then up at the neighboring line of disconsolate, low hills. "Ye-es, it is." His eyes came back and met Billy's deprecatingly, almost like those of a woman who feels that her youth and her charm have slipped behind her and who does not quite know whether she may still be worthy your attention. "Are you acquainted with this—this part of the country?"

"Well," Billy had got out his smoking material, from force of the habit with which a range-rider seizes every opportunity for a smoke, and singled meditatively a leaf. "Well, I kinda know it by sight, all right." And in his voice lurked a pride of knowledge inexplicable to one who has not known and loved the range-land. "I guess you'd have some trouble finding a square foot of it that I ain't been over," he added, mildly boastful.

If one might judge anything from a face as blank as that of a china doll, both the pride and the boastfulness were quite lost upon the stranger. Only his eyes were wistfully melancholy.

"My name is Alexander P. Dill," he informed Billy quite unnecessarily. "I was going to the Murton place. They told me it was only ten miles from town and it seems as though I must have taken the wrong road, somehow. Could you tell me about where it would be from here?"

Charming Billy's cupped hands hid his mouth, but his eyes laughed. "Roads ain't so plenty around here that you've any call to take one that don't belong to yuh," he reproved, when his cigarette was going well. "If Hardup's the place yuh started from, and if they headed yah right when they turned yuh loose, you've covered about eighteen miles and bent 'em into a beautiful quarter-circle—and how yuh ever went and done it undeliberate gets *me*. You are now seven miles from Hardup and sixteen miles, more or less, from Murton's." He stopped to watch the effect of his information.

Alexander P. Dill was a long man—an exceedingly long man, as Billy had already observed—and now he drooped so that he reminded Billy of shutting up a telescope. His mouth drooped, also, like that of a disappointed child, and his eyes took to themselves more melancholy. "I must have taken the wrong road," he repeated ineffectually.

"Yes," Billy agreed gravely, "I guess yuh must of; it does kinda look that way." There was no reason why he should feel anything more than a passing amusement at this wandering length of humanity, but Billy felt an unaccountable stirring of pity and a feeling of indulgent responsibility for the man.

"Could you—direct me to the right road?"

"Well, I reckon I could," Billy told him doubtfully, "but it would be quite a contract under the circumstances. Anyway, your cayuse is too near played; yuh better cut out your visit this time and come along back to town with me. You're liable to do a lot more wandering around till yuh find yourself plumb afoot." He did not know that he came near using the tone one takes toward a lost child.

"Perhaps, seeing I've come out of my way, I might as well," Mr. Dill decided hesitatingly. "That is, if you don't mind."

"Oh, I don't mind at all," Charming Billy assured him airily. "Uh course, I own this trail, and the less it's tracked up right now in its present state the better, but you're welcome to use it—if you're particular to trod soft and don't step in the middle."

Alexander P. Dill looked at him uncertainly, as if his sense of humor were weak and not to be trusted off-hand; turned his tired horse awkwardly in a way that betrayed an unfamiliarity with "neck-reining," and began to retrace his steps beside Charming Billy. His stirrups were too short, so that his knees were drawn up uncomfortably, and Billy, glancing sidelong down at them, wondered how the man could ride like that.

"You wasn't raised right around here, I reckon," Billy began amiably, when they were well under way.

"No—oh, no. I am from Michigan. I only came out West two weeks ago. I—I'm thinking some of raising wild cattle for the Eastern markets." Alexander P. Dill still had the wistful look in his eyes, which were unenthusiastically blue—just enough of the blue to make their color definite.

Charming Billy came near laughing, but some impulse kept him quiet-lipped and made his voice merely friendly. "Yes—this is a pretty good place for that business," he observed quite seriously. "A lot uh people are doing that same thing."

Mr. Dill warmed pitifully to the friendliness. "I was told that Mr. Murton wanted to sell his far—— ranch and cattle, and I was going to see him about it. I would like to buy a place outright, you see, with the cattle all branded, and—everything."

Billy suddenly felt the instinct of the champion. "Well, somebody lied to yuh a lot, then," he replied warmly. "Don't yuh never go near old Murton. In the first place, he ain't a cowman—he's a sheepman, on a small scale so far

"Kinda," Billy confirmed briefly.

"There seems to be a certain class-prejudice against strangers, out here. I can't understand it and I can't seem to get away from it. I believe those men deliberately misinformed me, for the sole reason that I am unfortunately a stranger and unfamiliar with the country. They do not seem to realize that this country must eventually be more fully developed, and that, in the very nature of things, strangers are sure to come and take advantage of the natural resources and aid materially in their development. I don't consider myself an interloper; I came here with the intention of making this my future home, and of putting every dollar of capital that I possess into this country; I wish I had more. I like the country; it isn't as if I came here to take something away. I came to add my mite; to help build up, not to tear down. And I can't understand the attitude of men who would maliciously—"

"It's kinda got to be part uh the scenery to josh a pilgrim," Billy took the trouble to explain. "We don't mean any harm. I reckon you'll get along all right, once yuh get wised up."

"Do you expect to be in town for any length of time?" Mr. Dill's voice was wistful, as well as his eyes. "Somehow, you don't seem to adopt that semi-hostile attitude, and I— I'm very glad for the opportunity of knowing you."

Charming Billy made a rapid mental calculation of his present financial resources and of past experience in the rate of depletion.

"Well. I may last a week or so, and I might pull out to-morrow," he decided candidly. "It all depends on the kinda luck I have."

Mr. Dill looked at him inquiringly, but he made no remark that would betray curiosity. "I have rented a room in a little house in the quietest part of town. The hotel isn't very clean and there is too much noise and drinking going on at night. I couldn't sleep there. I should be glad to have you share my room with me while you stay in town, if you will. It is clean and quiet."

Charming Billy turned his head and looked at him queerly; at his sloping shoulders, melancholy face and round, wistful eyes, and finally at the awkward, hunched-up knees of him. Billy did not mind night noises and drinking—to be truthful, they were two of the allurements which had brought him townward—and whether a room were clean or not troubled him little; he would not see much of it. His usual procedure while in town would, he suspected, seem very loose to Alexander P. Dill. It consisted chiefly of spending the nights where the noise clamored loudest and of sleeping during the day—sometimes—where was the most convenient spot to lay the length of him. He smiled whimsically at the contrast between them and their habits of living.

"Much obliged," he said. "I expect to be some busy, but maybe I'll drop in and bed down with yuh; once I hit town, it's hard to tell what I may do."

"I hope you'll feel perfectly free to come at any time and make yourself at home," Mr. Dill urged lonesomely.

"Sure. There's the old burg—I do plumb enjoy seeing the sun making gold on a lot uh town windows, like that over there. It sure looks good, when you've been living by your high lonesome and not seeing any window shine but your own little six-by-eight. Huh?"

"I—I must admit I like better to see the sunset turn my own windows to gold," observed Mr. Dill softly. "I haven't any, now; I sold the old farm when mother died. I was born and raised there. The woods pasture was west of the house, and every evening when I drove up the cows, and the sun was setting, the kitchen windows—"

Alexander P. Dill stopped very abruptly, and Billy, stealing a glance at his face, turned his own quickly away and gazed studiously at a bald hilltop off to the left. So finely tuned was his sympathy that for one fleeting moment he saw a homely, hilly farm in Michigan, with rail fences and a squat old house with wide porch and hard-beaten path from the kitchen door to the well and on to the stables; and down a long slope that was topped with great old trees, Alexander P. Dill shambling contentedly, driving with a crooked stick three mild-mannered old cows. "The blamed chump—what did he go and pull out for?" he asked himself fretfully. Then aloud: "I'm going to have a heart-to-heart talk with the cook at the hotel, and If he don't give us a real old round-up beefsteak, flopped over on the bare stovelids, there'll be things happen I'd hate to name over. He can sure do the business, all right; he used to cook for the Double-Crank. And you," he turned, elaborately cheerful, to Mr. Dill, "you are my guest."

"Thank you," smiled Mr. Dill, recovering himself and never guessing how strange was the last sentence to the lips of Charming Billy Boyle. "I shall be very glad to be the guest of somebody—once more."

"Yuh poor old devil, yuh sure drifted a long ways off your home range," mused Billy. Out loud he only emphasized the arrangement with:

"Sure thing!"

CHAPTER VI.
"That's My Dill Pickle!"

Charming Billy Boyle was, to put it mildly, enjoying his enforced vacation very much. To tell the plain truth and tell it without the polish of fiction, he was hilariously moistened as to his gullet and he was not thinking of quitting yet; he had only just begun.

He was sitting on an end of the bar in the Hardtip Saloon, his hat as far back on his head as it could possibly be pushed with any hope of its staying there at all. He had a glass in one hand, a cigarette in the other, and he was raking his rowels rhythmically up and down the erstwhile varnished bar in buzzing accompaniment, the while he chanted with much enthusiasm:

"How old is she, Billy boy, Billy boy?

How old is she, charming Billy?

Twice six, twice seven,

Forty-nine and eleven—"

The bartender, wiping the bar after an unsteady sheepherder, was careful to leave a generous margin around the person of Charming Billy who was at that moment asserting with much emphasis:

"She's a young thing, and cannot leave her mother."

"Twice-six's-twelve, 'n' twice-seven's-four-r-teen, 'n' twelve 'n' fourteen's—er—twelve—'n'—fourteen—" The unsteady sheepherder was laboring earnestly with the problem. "She ain't no spring chicken, she ain't!" He laughed tipsily, and winked up at the singer, but Billy was not observing him and his mathematical struggles. He refreshed himself from the glass, leaving the contents perceptibly lower—it was a large, thick glass with a handle, and it had flecks of foam down the inside—took a pull at the cigarette and inquired plaintively:

"Can she brew, can she bake, Billy boy, Billy boy?
Can she brew, can she bake, charming Billy?"

Another long pull at the cigarette, and then the triumphant declaration:

"She can brew n' she can bake,
She can sew n' she can make—
She's a young thing, and cannot leave her mother."

"She ain't s' young!" bawled the sheepherder, who was taking it all very seriously. "Say them numbers over again, onc't. Twelve-'n'-fourteen—"

"Aw, go off and lay down!" advised Charming Billy, in a tone of deep disgust. He was about to pursue still farther his inquiry into the housewifely qualifications of the mysterious "young thing," and he hated interruptions.

"Can she make a punkin pie, Billy boy, Billy boy?
Can she make a punkin pie, charming Billy?"

The door opened timidly and closed again, but he did not see who entered. He was not looking; he was holding the empty, foam-flecked glass behind him imperatively, and he was watching over his shoulder to see that the bartender did not skimp the filling and make it two-thirds foam. The bartender was punctiliously lavish, so that a crest of foam threatened to deluge the hand of Charming Billy and quite occupied him for the moment. When he squared himself again and buzzed his spurs against the bar, his mind was wholly given to the proper execution of the musical gem.

"She can make a punkin pie,

Quick's a cat can wink her eye—"

Something was going on, over in the dimly lighted corner near the door. Half a dozen men had grouped themselves there with their backs to Billy and they were talking and laughing; but the speech of them was an unintelligible clamor and their laughter a commingling roar. Billy gravely inspected his cigarette, which had gone cold, set down the glass and sought diligently for a match.

"Aw, come on an' have one on me!" bawled a voice peremptorily. "Yuh can't raise no wild cattle around *this* joint, lessen yuh wet up good with whisky. Why, a feller as long as you be needs a good jolt for every foot of yuh—and that's about fifteen when you're lengthened out good. Come on—don't be a damn' chubber! Yuh got to sample m' hospitality. Hey, Tom! set out about a quart uh your *mildest* for Daffy-down-Dilly. He's dry, clean down to his hand-made socks."

Charming Billy, having found a match, held it unlighted in his fingers and watched the commotion from his perch on the bar. In the very midst of the clamor towered the melancholy Alexander P. Dill, and he was endeavoring to explain, in his quiet, grammatical fashion. A lull that must have been an accident carried the words clearly across to Charming Billy.

"Thank you, gentlemen. I really don't care for anything in the way of refreshment. I merely came in to find a friend who has promised to spend the night with me. It is getting along toward bedtime. Have your fun, gentlemen, if you must—but I am really too tired to join you."

"Make 'im dance!" yelled the sheepherder, giving over the attempt to find the sum of twelve and fourteen. "By gosh, yuh made *me* dance when I struck town. Make 'im dance!"

"You go off and lay down!" commanded Billy again, and to emphasize his words leaned and emptied the contents of his glass neatly inside the collar of the sheepherder. "Cool down, yuh Ba-ba-black-sheep!"

The herder forgot everything after that—everything but the desire to tear limb from limb one Charming Billy Boyle, who sat and raked his spurs up and down the marred front of the bar and grinned maliciously down at him. "Go-awn off, before I take yuh all to pieces," he urged wearily, already regretting the unjustifiable waste of good beer. "Quit your buzzing; I wanta listen over there."

"Come on 'n' have a drink!" vociferated the hospitable one. "Yuh got to be sociable, or yuh can't stop in *this* man's town." So insistent was he that he laid violent hold of Mr. Dill and tried to pull him bodily to the bar.

"Gentlemen, this passes a joke!" protested Mr. Dill, looking around him in his blankly melancholy way. "I do not drink liquor. I must insist upon your stopping this horseplay immediately!"

"Oh, it ain't no *play*," asserted the insistent one darkly. "I mean it, by thunder."

It was at this point that Charming Billy decided to have a word. "Here, break away, there!" he yelled, pushing the belligerent sheepherder to one side. "Hands off that long person! That there's *my* dill pickle!"

Mr. Dill was released, and Billy fancied hazily that it was because he so ordered; as a matter of fact, Mr. Dill, catching sight of him there, had thrown the men and their importunities off as though they had been rough-mannered boys. He literally plowed his way through them and stopped deprecatingly before Billy.

"It is getting late," he observed, mildly reproachful. "I thought I would show you the way to my room, if you don't mind."

Billy stared down at him. "Well, I'm going to be busy for a while yet," he demurred. "I've got to lick this misguided son-of-a-gun that's blatting around wanting to eat me alive—and I got my eyes on your friend in the rear, there, that's saying words about you, Dilly. Looks to me like I'm going to be some occupied for quite a spell. You run along to bed and don't yuh bother none about *me*."

"The matter is not so urgent but what I can wait until you are ready," Mr. Dill told him quietly, but with decision. He folded his long arms and ranged himself patiently alongside Billy. And Billy, regarding him uneasily, felt convinced that though he tarried until the sun returned Mr. Dill would stand right there and wait—like a well-broken range-horse when the reins are dropped to the ground. Charming Billy did not know why it made him uncomfortable, but it did and he took immediate measures to relieve the sensation.

He turned fretfully and cuffed the clamorous sheepherder, who seemed to lack the heart for actual hostilities but indulged in much recrimination and was almost in tears. "Aw, shut up!" growled Billy. "A little more uh that war-talk and I'll start in and learn yuh some manners. I don't want any more of it. Yuh hear?"

It is a fact that trifles sometimes breed large events. Billy, to make good his threat, jumped off the bar. In doing so he came down upon the toes of Jack Morgan, the hospitable soul who had insisted upon treating Mr. Dill and who had just come up to renew the argument. Jack Morgan was a man of uncertain temper and he also had toes exceedingly tender. He struck out, missed Billy, who was thinking only of the herder, and it looked quite as though the blow was meant for Mr. Dill.

After that, things happened quickly and with some confusion. Others became active, one way or the other, and the clamor was great, so that it was easily heard down the street and nearly emptied the other saloons.

When the worst of it was over and one could tell for a certainty what was taking place, Charming Billy was holding a man's face tightly against the bar and was occasionally beating it with his fist none too gently. Mr. Dill, an arm's length away, had Jack Morgan and one other offender clutched by the neck in either hand and he

53

was solemnly and systematically butting their heads together until they howled. The bartender had just succeeded in throwing the sheepherder out through the back door, and he was wiping his hands and feeling very well satisfied with himself.

"I'd oughta fired him long ago, when he first commenced building trouble," he remarked, to no one in particular. "The darned lamb-licker—he's broke and has been all evening. I don't know what made me stand for 'im long as I did."

Billy, moved perhaps by weariness rather than mercy, let go his man and straightened up, feeling mechanically for his hat. His eyes met those of the melancholy Mr. Dill.

"If you're quite through"—bang! went the heads— "perhaps we may as well"—bang!—"leave this unruly crowd"—bang!!—"and go to our room. It is after eleven o'clock." Mr. Dill looked as though his present occupation was unpleasant but necessary and as though, to please Billy, he could keep it up indefinitely.

Charming Billy stood quite still, staring at the other and at what he was doing; and while he stared and wondered, something came into the heart of him and quite changed his destiny. He did not know what it was, or why it was so; at the time he realized only a deep amazement that Mr. Dill, mild of manner, correct of speech and wistful-eyed, should be standing there banging the heads of two men who were considered rather hard to handle. Certainly Jack Morgan was reputed a "bad actor" when it came to giving blows. And while Alexander P. Dill was a big man—

an enormous man, one might say—he had none of the earmarks of a fighting man. It was, perhaps, his very calmness that won Billy for good and all. Before, Charming Billy had felt toward him a certain amused pity; his instinct had been to protect Mr. Dill. He would never feel just that way again; Mr. Dill, it would seem, was perfectly well able to protect himself.

"Shall we go?" Mr. Dill poised the two heads for another bang and held them so. By this time every one in the room was watching, but he had eyes only for Billy.

"Just as you say," Billy assented submissively.

Mr. Dill shook the two with their faces close together, led them to a couple of chairs and set them emphatically down. "Now, see if you can behave yourselves," he advised, in the tone a father would have used toward two refractory boys. "You have been acting boorishly and disgracefully all evening. It was you who directed me wrong, to-day. You have not, at any time since I first met you, acted like gentlemen; I should be sorry to think this country held many such brainless louts." He turned inquiringly toward Charming Billy and nodded his head toward the door. Billy, stooping unsteadily for his hat which he discovered under his feet, followed him meekly out.

CHAPTER VII.
"Till Hell's a Skating-rink."

Charming Billy opened his eyes slowly, but with every sense at the normal degree of alertness; which was a way he had, born of light sleeping and night-watching. He had slept heavily, from the feel of his head, and he remembered the unwisdom of drinking four glasses of whisky and then changing irresponsibly to beer. He had not undressed, it would seem, and he was lying across the middle of a bed with his spurred boots hanging over the edge. A red comforter had been thrown across him, and he wondered why. He looked around the room and discovered Mr. Dill seated in a large, cane rocker—which was unquestionably not big enough for his huge person—his feet upon another chair and his hands folded inertly on his drawn-up knees. He was asleep, with his head lying against the chair-back and his face more melancholy than ever and more wistful. His eyes, Billy observed, were deep-sunk and dark-ringed. He sat up suddenly—did Billy, and threw off the cover with some vehemence. "Darn me for a drunken chump!" he exclaimed, and clanked over to the chair.

"Here, Dilly"—to save the life of him he could not refrain from addressing him so—"why in thunder didn't yuh kick me awake, and make me get off your bed? What did yuh let me do it for—and you setting up all night—oh, this is sure a hell of a note!"

Mr. Dill opened his eyes, stared blankly and came back from his dreaming. "You were so—so impatient when I tried to get you up," he explained in a tired voice. "And you had a way of laying your hands on your revolver when I insisted. It seems you took me for a shepherd and were very unfriendly; so I thought it best to let you stay as you were, but I'm afraid you were not very comfortable. One can rest so much better between sheets. You would not," he added plaintively, "even permit me to take your boots off for you."

Charming Billy sat down upon the edge of the bed, all tousled as he was, and stared abstractedly at Mr. Dill. Perhaps he had never before felt so utterly disgusted with himself, or realized so keenly his shortcomings. Not even the girl had humbled him so completely as had this long, lank, sinfully grammatical man from Michigan.

"You've sure got me where I live, Dilly," he said slowly and haltingly, feeling mechanically for the makings of a smoke. "Charming Billy Boyle ain't got a word to say for himself. But if yuh ain't plumb sick and disgusted with the spectacle I've made uh myself, yuh can count on me till hell's a skating-rink. I ain't always thisaway. I do have spells when I'm some lucid."

It was not much, but such as it was it stood for his oath of allegiance.

Alexander P. Dill sat up straight, his long, bony fingers— which Billy could still mentally see gripping the necks of those two in the saloon—lying loosely upon the chair-arms. "I hope you will not mention the matter again," he said. "I realize that this is not Michigan, and that the temptations are—But we will not discuss it. I shall be very grateful for your friendship, and—"

"Grateful!" snorted Billy, spilling tobacco on the strip of faded ingrain carpet before the bed. "Grateful—hell!"

Mr. Dill looked at him a moment and there was a certain keen man-measuring behind the wistfulness. But he said no more about the friendship of Charming Billy Boyle, which was as well.

That is why the two of them later sat apart on the sunny side of the hotel "office"—which was also a saloon—and talked of many things, but chiefly of the cattle industry as Montana knows it and of the hopes and the aims of Alexander P. Dill. Perhaps, also, that is why Billy breathed clean of whisky and had the bulk of his winter wages still unspent in his pocket.

"Looks to me," he was saying between puffs, "like you'd uh stayed back where yuh knew the lay uh the land, instead uh drifting out here where it's all plumb strange to yuh."

"Well, several incidents influenced my actions," Mr. Dill explained quietly. "I had always lived within twenty miles of my birthplace. I owned a general store in a little place near the old farm, and did well. The farm paid well, also. Then mother died and the place did not seem quite the same. A railroad was built through the town and the land I owned there rose enormously in value. I had a splendid location for a modern store but I could not seem to make up my mind to change. So I sold out everything—store, land, the home farm and all, and received a good figure—a *very* good figure. I was very fortunate in owning practically the whole townsite—the new townsite, that is. I do not like these so-called booms, however, and so I left to begin somewhere else. I did not care to enter the mercantile business again, and our doctor advised me to live as much as possible in the open air. Mother died of consumption. So I decided to come West and buy a cattle ranch. I believed I should like it. I always liked animals."

"Uh-huh—so do I." It was not just what Charming Billy most wanted to say, but that much was perfectly safe, and noncommittal to say.

Mr. Dill was silent a minute, looking speculatively across to the Hardup Saloon which was practically empty and therefore quite peaceful. Billy, because long living on the range made silence easy, smoked and said nothing.

"Mr. Boyle," began Dill at last, in the hesitating way that he had used when Billy first met him, "you say you know this country, and have worked at cattle-raising for a good many years—"

"Twelve," supplemented Charming Billy. "Turned my first cow when I was sixteen."

"So you must be perfectly familiar with the business. I frankly admit that I am not familiar with it. You say you are at present out of employment and so I am thinking seriously of offering you a position myself, as confidential adviser if you like. I really need some one who can accompany me about the country and keep me from such deplorable blunders as was yesterday's experience. After I have bought a place, I shall need some one who is familiar with the business and will honestly work for my interests and assist me in the details until I have myself gained a practical working-knowledge of it. I think I can make such an arrangement to your advantage as well as my own. From the start the salary would be what is usually paid to a foreman. What do you say?"

For an appreciable space Charming Billy Boyle did not say a word. He was not stupid and he saw in a flash all the possibilities that lay in the offer. To be next the very top— to have his say in the running of a model cow-outfit—and it should be a model outfit if he took charge, for he had ideas of his own about how these things should be done— to be foreman, with the right to "hire and fire" at his own discretion—He turned, flushed and bright-eyed, to Dill.

"God knows why yuh cut *me* out for the job," he said in a rather astonished voice. "What you've seen uh me, so far, ain't been what I'd call a gilt-edge recommend. But if you're fool enough to mean it serious, it's as I told yuh a while back: Yuh can count on me till they're cutting figure-eights all over hell."

"That, according to the scientists who are willing to concede the existence of such a place, will be quite as long as I shall be likely to have need of your loyalty," observed Mr. Dill, puckering his long face into the first smile Billy had seen him attempt.

He did not intimate the fact that he had inquired very closely into the record and the general range qualifications of Charming Billy Boyle, sounding, for that purpose, every responsible man in Hardup. With the new-born respect for him bred by his peculiarly efficacious way of handling those who annoyed him beyond the limit, he was told the truth and recognized it as such. So he was not really as rash and as given over to his impulses as Billy, in his ignorance of the man, fancied.

The modesty of Billy would probably have been shocked if he had heard the testimony of his fellows concerning him. As it was, he was rather dazed and a good deal inclined to wonder how Alexander P. Dill had ever managed to accumulate enough capital to start anything—let alone a cow-outfit—if he took on trust every man he met. He privately believed that Dill had taken a long chance, and that he should consider himself very lucky because he had accidentally picked a man who would not "steal him blind."

After that there were many days of riding to and fro, canvassing all northern Montana in search of a location and an outfit that suited them and that could be bought. And in the riding, Mr. Dill became under the earnest tutelage of Charming Billy a shade less ignorant of range ways and of the business of "raising wild cattle for the Eastern markets."

He even came to speak quite easily of "outfits" in all the nice shades of meaning which are attached to that hard-worked term. He could lay the saddle-blanket smooth and unwrinkled, slap the saddle on and cinch it without fixing it either upon the withers or upon the rump of his long-suffering mount. He could swing his quirt without damaging his own person, and he rode with his stirrups where they should be to accommodate the length of him—all of which speaks eloquently of the honest intentions of Dill's confidential adviser.

CHAPTER VIII.
Just a Day-dream.

Charming Billy rode humped over the saddle-horn, as rides one whose mind feels the weight of unpleasant thoughts. Twice he had glanced uncertainly at his companion, opening his lips for speech; twice he had closed them silently and turned again to the uneven trail.

Mr. Dill also was humped forward in the saddle, but if one might judge from his face it was because he was cold. The wind blew chill from out the north and they were facing it; the trail they followed was frozen hard and the gray clouds above promised snow. The cheek-bones of Dill were purple and the point of his long nose was very red. Tears stood in his eyes, whipped there by the biting wind.

"How far are we now from town?" he asked dispiritedly.

"Only about five miles," Billy cheered. Then, as if trivial speech had made easier what he had in mind to say, he turned resolutely toward the other. "Yuh expect to meet old man Robinson there, don't yuh?"

"That was the arrangement, as I understood it"

"And you're thinking strong of buying him out?"

"His place appeals to me more than any of the others, and—yes, it seems to me that I can't do better." Mr. Dill turned the collar of his coat up a bit farther—or fancied he did so—and looked questioningly at Billy.

"Yuh gave me leave to advise yuh where yuh needed it," Billy said almost challengingly, "and I'm going to call yuh, right here and now. If yuh take my advice yuh won't go making medicine with old Robinson any more. He'll do yuh, sure. He's asking yuh double what the outfit's worth. They *all* are. It looks to me like they think you're just out here to get rid of your pile and the bigger chunk they can pry loose from yuh the better. I was going to put yuh next before this, only yuh didn't seem to take to any uh the places real serious, so it wasn't necessary."

"I realize that one cannot buy land and cattle for nothing," Dill chuckled. "It seemed to me that, compared with the prices others have asked, Mr. Robinson's offer was very reasonable."

"It may be lower than Jacobs and Wilter, but that don't make it right."

"Well, there were the Two Sevens"—he meant the Seventy-Seven, but that was a mere detail—"I didn't get to see the owner, you know. I have written East, however, and should hear from him in a few days."

"Yuh ain't likely to do business with *that* layout, because I don't believe they'd sell at any price. Old Robinson is the washout yuh want to ride around at present; I ain't worrying about the rest, right now. He's a smooth old devil, and he'll do yuh sure."

To this Mr. Dill made no reply whatever. He fumbled the fastenings on his coon-skin coat, tried to pull his cap lower and looked altogether unhappy. And Charming Billy, not at ail sure that his advice would be taken or his warning heeded, stuck the spurs into his horse and set a faster pace reflecting gloomily upon the trials of being confidential adviser to one who, in a perfectly mild and good-mannered fashion, goes right along doing pretty much as he pleases.

It made him think, somehow, of Miss Bridger and the way she had forced him to take his gun with him when he had meant to leave it. She was like Dill in that respect: nice and good-natured and smiling—only Dill smiled but seldom—and yet always managing to make you give up your own wishes. He wished vaguely that the wanderings of Dill would bring them back to the Double-Crank country, instead of leading them always farther afield. He did not, however, admit openly to himself that he wanted to see Miss Bridger again; yet he did permit himself to wonder if she ever played coon-can with any one else, or if she had already forgotten the game. Probably she had, and—well, a good many other things that he remembered quite distinctly.

Later, when they had reached town, were warmed and fed and when even Billy was thinking seriously of sleep, Dill came over and sat down beside him solemnly, folded his bony hands upon knees quite as bony, regarded pensively the generously formed foot dangling some distance before him and smiled his puckered smile.

"I have been wondering, William, if you had not some plan of your own concerning this cattle-raising business, which you think is better than mine but which you hesitate to express. If you have, I hope you will feel quite free to—er—lay it before the head of the firm. It may interest you to know that I have, as you would put it, 'failed to connect' with Mr. Robinson. So, if you have any ideas—"

"Oh, I'm burning up with 'em," Charming Billy retorted in a way he meant to be sarcastic, but which Mr. Dill took quite seriously.

"Then I hope you won't hesitate—"

"Now look here, Dilly," expostulated he, between puffs. "Recollect, it's *your* money that's going to feed the birds— and it's your privilege to throw it out to suit yourself. Uh course, I might day-dream about the way I'd start into the cow-business if I was a millionaire—"

"I'm not a millionaire," Mr. Dill hastened to correct. "A couple of hundred thousand or so, is about all—"

"Well, a fellow don't have to pin himself down to just so many dollars and cents—not when he's building himself a pet dream. And if a fellow dreams about starting up an outfit of his own, it don't prove he'd make it stick in reality." The tone of Billy, however, did not express any doubt.

Mr. Dill untangled his legs, crossed them the other way and regarded the other dangling foot. "I should like very much," he hinted mildly, "to have you tell me this—er— day-dream, as you call it."

So Charming Billy, tilted back in his chair and watching with half-shut eyes the intangible smoke-wreath from his cigarette, found words for his own particular air-castle which he had builded on sunny days when the Double-Crank herds grazed peacefully around him; or on stormy nights when he sat alone in the line-camp and played solitaire with the mourning wind crooning accompaniment; or on long rides alone, when the trail was plain before him and the grassland stretched away and away to a far sky-line, and the white clouds sailed sleepily over his head and about him the meadowlarks sang. And while he found the words, he somehow forgot Dill, long and lean and lank, listening beside him, and spoke more freely than he had meant to do when Dill first opened the subject a few minutes before.

"Recollect, this is just a day-dream," he began. "But, if I was a millionaire, or if I had two hundred thousand dollars—and to me they don't sound much different—I'd sure start a cow-outfit right away immediately at once. But I wouldn't buy out nobody; I'd go right back and start like they did—if they're real old-timers. I'd go down south into Texas and I'd buy me a bunch uh two-year-olds and bring 'em up here, and turn 'em loose on the best piece of open range I know—and I know a peach. In a year or so I'd go back and do the same again, and I'd keep it up whilst my money held out I'd build me a home ranch back somewheres in a draw in the hills, where there's lots uh water and lots uh shelter, and I'd get a bunch uh men that savvied cow-brutes, put 'em on horses that wouldn't trim down their self-respect every time they straddled 'em, and then I'd just ride around and watch myself get rich. And—" He stopped and dreamed silently over his cigarette.

"And then?" urged Mr. Dill, after a moment.

"And then—I'd likely get married, and raise a bunch uh boys to carry on the business when I got old and fat, and too damn' lazy to ride off a walk."

Mr. Dill took three minutes to weigh the matter. Then, musingly: "I'm not sure about the boys. I'm not a marrying man, myself—but just giving a snap judgment on the other part of it, I will say it sounds—well, feasible."

CHAPTER IX.
The "Double-Crank."

The weeks that followed immediately after bulged big with the things which Billy must do or have done. For to lie on one's back in the sun with one's hat pulled low, dreaming lazily and with minute detail the perfect supervision of a model cow-outfit from its very inception up through the buying of stock and the building of corrals and the breaking of horses to the final shipping of great trainloads of sleek beef, is one thing; to start out in reality to do all that, with the hundred little annoyances and hindrances which come not to one's dreaming in the sun, is something quite different.

But with all the perplexities born of his changed condition and the responsibility it brought him, Billy rejoiced in the work and airily planned the years to come—years in which he would lead Alexander P. Dill straight into the ranks of the Western millionaires; years when the sun of prosperity would stand always straight overhead, himself a Joshua who would, by his uplifted hands, keep it there with never a cloud to dim the glory of its light.

For the first time in his life he rode over Texas prairies and lost thereby some ideals and learned many things, the while he spent more money than he had ever owned—or ever expected to own—as the preliminary to making his pet dream come true; truth to tell, it mattered little to Billy Boyle whether his dream came true for himself or for another, so long as he himself were the chief magician.

So it was with a light heart that he swung down from the train at Tower, after his homing flight, and saw Dill, conspicuous as a flagstaff, waiting for him on the platform, his face puckered into a smile of welcome and his bony fingers extended ready to grip painfully the hand of Charming Billy.

"I'm very glad to see you back, William," he greeted earnestly. "I hope you are well, and that you met with no misfortune while you were away. I have been very anxious for your return, as I need your advice upon a matter which seems to me of prime importance. I did not wish to make any decisive move until I had consulted with you, and time is pressing. Did you—er—buy as many cattle as you expected to get?" It seemed to Billy that there was an anxious note in his voice. "Your letters were too few and too brief to keep me perfectly informed of your movements."

"Why, everything was lovely at my end uh the trail, Dilly—only I fell down on them four thousand two-year-olds. Parts uh the country was quarantined for scab, and I went way around them places. And I was too late to see the cattlemen in a bunch when they was at the Association—only you ain't likely to savvy that part uh the business—and had to chase 'em all over the country. Uh course it was my luck to have 'em stick their prices up on the end of a pole, where I didn't feel like climbing after 'em. So I only contracted for a couple uh thousand to be laid down in Billings somewhere between the first and the tenth of June, at twenty-one dollars a head. It was the best I could do this year—but next winter I can go down earlier, before the other buyers beat me to it, and do a lot better. Don't yuh worry, Dilly; it ain't serious."

On the contrary, Dill looked relieved, and Billy could not help noticing it. His own face clouded a little. Perhaps Dill had lost his money, or the bulk of it, and they couldn't do all the things they had meant to do, after all; how else, thought Billy uneasily, could he look like that over what should ordinarily be something of a disappointment? He remembered that Dill, after the workings of the cattle business from the very beginning had been painstakingly explained to him just before Billy started south, had been anxious to get at least four thousand head of young stock on the range that spring. Something must have gone wrong. Maybe a bank had gone busted or something like that. Billy stole a glance up at the other, shambling silently along beside him, and decided that something had certainly happened—and on the heels of that he remembered oddly that he had felt almost exactly like this when Miss Bridger had asked him to show her where was the coffee, and there *wasn't* any coffee. There was the same heavy feeling in his chest, and the same—

"I wrote you a letter three or four days ago—on the third, to be exact," Dill was saying. "I don't suppose it reached you, however. I was going to have you meet me in Hardup; but then your telegram was forwarded to me there and I came on here at once. I only arrived this morning. I think that after we have something to eat we would better start out immediately, unless you have other plans. I drove over in a rig, and as the horses have rested several hours and are none the worse for the drive, I think we can easily make the return trip this afternoon."

"You're the doctor," assented Billy briefly, more uneasy than before and yet not quite at the point of asking questions. In his acquaintance with Dill he had learned that it was not always wise to question too closely; where Dill wished to give his confidence he gave it freely, but beyond the limit he had fixed for himself was a stone wall, masked by the flowers, so to speak, of his unfailing courtesy. Billy had once or twice inadvertently located that wall.

A great depression seized upon him and made him quite indifferent to the little pleasures of homecoming; of seeing the grass green and velvety and hearing the familiar notes of the meadow-larks and the curlews. The birds had not returned when he went away, and now the air was musical with them. Driving over the prairies seemed fairly certain of being anything but pleasant to-day, with Dill doubled awkwardly in the seat beside him, carrying on an intermittent monologue of trivial stuff to which Billy scarcely listened. He could feel that there was something at the back of it all, and that was enough for him at present. He was not even anxious now to hear just what was the form of the disaster which had overtaken them.

"While you were away," Dill began at last in the tone that braces one instinctively for the worst, "I met accidentally a man of whom I had heard, but whom I had not seen. In the course of our casual conversation he discovered that I was about to launch myself and my capital into the cattle-business, whereupon he himself made me an offer which I felt should not be lightly brushed aside."

"They all did!" Billy could not help flinging out half-resentfully, when he remembered that but for his timely interference Dill would have been gulled more than once.

"I admit that in my ignorance some offers advantageous only to those who made them appealed to me strongly. But I believe you will agree with me that this is different. In this case I am offered a full section of land, with water-rights, buildings, corrals, horses, wagons and all improvements necessary to the running of a good outfit, and ten thousand head of mixed cattle, just as they are now running loose on the range, for three hundred thousand dollars. I need only pay half this amount down, a five-year mortgage at eight per cent. on the property covering the remainder, to be paid in five yearly installments, falling due after shipping time. Now that you did not buy as much young stock as we at first intended, I can readily make the first payment on this place and have left between ten and twelve thousand dollars to carry us along until we begin to get some returns from the investment I am anxious to have you look over the proposition, and tell me what you think of it. If you are in favor of buying, we can have immediate possession; ten days after the deal is closed, I think the man said."

Billy tilted his hat-brim a bit to keep the sun from his eyes, and considered gravely the proposition. It was a great relief to discover that his fears were groundless and that it was only another scheme of Dilly's; another snare which he, perhaps, would be compelled, in Dill's interest, to move aside. He put the reins down between his knees and gripped them tightly while he made a cigarette. It was not until he was pinching the end shut that he spoke.

"If it's as you say"—and he meant no offense—"it looks like a good thing, all right. But yuh can't most always tell. I'd have to see it—say, yuh might tell me where this bonanza is, and what's the name uh the brand. If it's anywheres around here I ought to know the place, all right."

Alexander P. Dill must, after all, have had some sense of humor; his eyes lost their melancholy enough almost to twinkle. "Well, the owner's name is Brown," he said slowly. "I believe they call the brand the Double-Crank. It is located—"

"Located—hell!—do yuh think *I* don't know?" The cigarette, ready to light as it was, slipped from Billy's fingers and dropped unheeded over the wheel to the brown trail below. He took the reins carefully from between his knees, straightened one that had become twisted and turned out upon the prairie to avoid a rough spot where a mud-puddle had dried in hard ridges. Beyond, he swung back again, leaned and flicked an early horse-fly from the ribs of the off-horse, touched the other one up a bit with his whip and settled back at ease, tilting his hat at quite another angle.

"Oh, where have yuh been, Billy boy, Billy boy?
Oh, where have yuh been, charming Billy?"

He hummed, in a care-free way that would have been perfectly maddening to any one with nerves.

"I suppose I am to infer from your silence that you do not take kindly to the proposition," observed Mr. Dill, in a colorless tone which betrayed the fact that he did have nerves.

"I can take a josh, all right," Billy stopped singing long enough to say. "For a steady-minded cuss, yuh do have surprising streaks, Dilly, and that's a fact. Yuh sprung it on me mighty smooth, for not having much practice—I'll say that for yuh."

Mr. Dill looked hurt. "I hope you do not seriously think that I would joke upon a matter of business," he protested.

"Well, I know old Brown pretty tolerable well—and I ain't accusing him uh ribbing up a big josh on yuh. He ain't that brand."

"I must confess I fail to get your point of view," said Mr. Dill, with just a hint of irascibility in his voice. "There is no joke unless you are forcing one upon me now. Mr. Brown made me a bona-fide offer, and I have made a small deposit to hold it until you came and I could consult you. We have three days left in which to decide for or against it. It is all perfectly straight, I assure you."

Billy took time to consider this possibility. "Well, in that case, and all jokes aside, I'd a heap rather have the running uh the Double-Crank than be President and have all the newspapers hollering how 'President Billy Boyle got up at eight this morning and had ham-and-eggs for his breakfast, and then walked around the block with the Queen uh England hanging onto his left arm,' or anything like that But what I can't seem to get percolated through me is why, in God's name, the Double-Crank wants to sell."

"That," Mr. Dill remarked, his business instincts uppermost, "it seems to me, need not concern us—seeing that they *will* sell, and at a price we can handle."

"I reckon you're right. Would yuh mind saying over the details uh the offer again?"

"Mr. Brown"—Dill cleared his throat—"offered to sell me a full section of land, extending from the line-fence of the home ranch, east—"

"Uh-huh—now what the devil's his idea in that?" Billy cut in earnestly. "The Double-Crank owns about three or four miles uh bottom land, up the creek west uh the home ranch. Wonder why he wants to hold that out?"

"I'm sure I do not know," answered Dill. "He did not mention that to me, but confined himself, naturally, to what he was willing to sell."

"Oh it don't matter. And all the range stuff, yuh said—ten thousand head, and—"

"I believe he is reserving some thoroughbred stock which he has bought in the last year or two. The stock on the range—the regular range grade-stock—all goes, as well as the saddle-horses."

"Must be the widow said yes and wants him to settle down and be a gentle farmer," decided Billy after a moment.

"We will meet him in Hardup to-night or to-morrow," Dill observed, as if he were anxious to decide the matter finally. "Do you think we would better buy?" It was one of his little courteous ways to say "we" in discussing a business transaction, just as though Billy were one of the firm.

"Buy? You bet your life we'll buy! I wisht the papers was all signed up and in your inside pocket right now, Dilly. I'm going to get heart failure the worst kind if there's any hitch. Lord, what luck!"

"Then, we will consider the matter as definitely settled," said Dill, with a sigh of satisfaction. "Brown cannot rescind now—there is my deposit to bind the bargain. I will say I should have been sorely disappointed if you had not shown that you favored the idea. It seems to me to be just what we want."

"Oh—that part. But it seems to *me* that old Brown is sure locoed to give us a chance at the outfit. He's gone plumb silly. His friends oughta appoint a guardian over him—only I hope they won't get action till this deal is cinched tight." With that, Billy relapsed into crooning his ditty. But there were odd breaks when he stopped short in the middle of a line and forgot to finish, and there was more than one cigarette wasted by being permitted to go cold and then being chewed abstractedly until it nearly fell to pieces.

Beside him, Alexander P. Dill, folded loosely together in the seat, caressed his knees and stared unseeingly at the trail ahead of them and said never a word for more than an hour.

CHAPTER X.
The Day We Celebrate.

The days that followed were to Billy much like a delicious dream. Sometimes he stopped short and wondered uneasily if he would wake up pretty soon to find that he was still an exile from the Double-Crank, wandering with Dill over the country in search of a location. Sometimes he laughed aloud unexpectedly, and said, "Hell!" in a chuckling undertone when came fresh realization of the miracle. But mostly he was an exceedingly busy young man, with hands and brain too full of the stress of business to do much wondering.

They were in possession of the Double-Crank, now—he in full charge, walking the path which his own feet, when he was merely a "forty-dollar puncher," had helped wear deep to the stable and corrals; giving orders where he had been wont to receive them; riding horses which he had long completed, but which had heretofore been kept sacred to the use of Jawbreaker and old Brown himself; eating and sleeping in the house with Dill instead of making one of the crowd in the bunk-house; ordering the coming and going of the round-up crew and tasting to the full the joys—and the sorrows—of being "head push" where he had for long been content to serve. Truly, the world had changed amazingly for one Charming Billy Boyle.

Most of the men he had kept on, for he liked them well and they had faith to believe that success would not spoil him. The Pilgrim he had promised himself the pleasure of firing bodily off the ranch within an hour of his first taking control—but the Pilgrim had not waited. He had left the ranch with the Old Man and where he had gone did not concern Billy at the time. For there was the shipment of young stock from the South to meet and drive up to the home range, and there was the calf round-up to start on time, and after all the red tape of buying the outfit and turning over the stock had been properly wound up, time was precious in the extreme through May and June and well into July.

But habit is strong upon a man even after the conditions which bred the habit have utterly changed. One privilege had been always kept inviolate at the Double-Crank, until it had come to be looked upon as an inalienable right. The Glorious Fourth had been celebrated, come rain, come shine. Usually the celebration was so generous that it did not stop at midnight; anywhere within a week was considered permissible, a gradual tapering off—not to say sobering up—being the custom with the more hilarious souls.

When Dill with much solemnity tore off June from the calendar in the dining room—the calendar with Custer's Last Charge rioting redly above the dates—Billy, home for a day from the roundup, realized suddenly that time was on the high lope; at least, that is how he put it to Dill.

"Say, Dilly, we sure got to jar loose from getting rich long enough to take in that picnic over to Bluebell Grove. Didn't know there was a picnic or a Bluebell Grove? Well now, there is. Over on Horned-Toad Creek—nice, pretty name to go with the grove, ain't it?—they've got a patch uh shade big over as my hat. Right back up on the hill is the schoolhouse where they do their dancing, and they've got a table or two and a swing for the kids to fall outa—and they call it Bluebell Grove because yuh never saw a bluebell within ten mile uh the place. That's where the general round-up for the Fourth is pulled off this year—so Jim Bleeker was telling me this morning. We sure got to be present, Dilly."

"I'm afraid I'm not the sort of man to shine in society, William," dissented the other modestly. "You can go, and—"

"Don't yuh never *dance*?" Billy eyed him speculatively. A man under fifty—and Dill might be anywhere between thirty and forty—who had two sound legs and yet did not dance!

"Oh, I used to, after a fashion. But my feet are so far off that I find communication with them necessarily slow, and they have a habit of embarking in wild ventures of their own. I do not believe they are really popular with the feminine element, William. And so I'd rather—"

"Aw, you'll have to go and try it a whirl, anyhow. We ain't any of us experts. Yuh see, the boys have been accustomed to having the wheels of industry stop revolving on the Fourth, and turning kinda wobbly for four or five days after. I don't feel like trying to break 'em in to keep on working—do you?"

"To use your own term," said Dill, suddenly reckless of his diction, "you're sure the doctor."

"Well, then, the proper dope for this case is, all hands show up at the picnic." He picked up his hat from the floor, slapped it twice against his leg to remove the dust, pinched the crown into four dents, set it upon his head at a jaunty angle and went out, singing softly:

"She's a young thing, and cannot leave her mother."

Dill, looking after him, puckered his face into what passed with him for a smile. "I wonder now," he meditated aloud, "if William is not thinking of some particular young lady who—er—who 'cannot leave her mother'." If he had only known it, William was; he was also wondering whether she would be at the picnic. And if she were at the picnic, would she remember him? He had only seen her that one night—and to him it seemed a very long while ago. He thought, however, that he might be able to recall himself to her mind—supposing she had forgotten. It was a long time ago, he kept reminding himself, and the light was poor and he hadn't shaved for a week—he had always afterward realized that with much mental discomfort—and he really did look a lot different when he had on his "war-togs," by which he meant his best clothes. He wouldn't blame her at all If she passed him up for a stranger, just at first. A great deal more he thought on the same subject, and quite as foolishly.

Because of much thinking on the subject, when he and Dill rode down the trail which much recent passing had made unusually dusty, with the hot sunlight of the Fourth making the air quiver palpably around them; with the cloudless blue arching hotly over their heads and with the four by six cotton flag flying an involuntary signal of distress—on account of its being hastily raised bottom-side-up and left that way—and beckoning them from the little clump of shade below, the heart of Charming Billy Boyle beat unsteadily under the left pocket of his soft, cream-colored silk shirt, and the cheeks of him glowed red under the coppery tan. Dill was not the sort of man who loves fast riding and they ambled along quite decorously— "like we was headed for prayer-meeting with a singing-book under each elbow," thought Billy, secretly resentful of the pace.

"I reckon there'll be quite a crowd," he remarked wistfully. "I see a good many horses staked out already."

Dill nodded absently, and Billy took to singing his pet ditty; one must do something when one is covering the last mile of a journey toward a place full of all sorts of delightful possibilities—and covering that mile at a shambling trot which is truly maddening.

"She can make a punkin pie quick's a cat can wink her eye,
She's a young thing, and cannot leave her mother!"

"But, of course," observed Mr. Dill quite unexpectedly, "you know, William, time will remedy that drawback."

Billy started, looked suspiciously at the other, grew rather red and shut up like a clam. He did more; he put the spurs to his horse and speedily hid himself in a dust-cloud, so

83

that Dill, dutifully keeping pace with him, made a rather spectacular arrival whether he would or no.

Charming Billy, his hat carefully dimpled, his blue tie fastidiously knotted and pierced with the Klondyke nugget-pin which was his only ornament, wandered hastily through the assembled groups and slapped viciously at mosquitoes. Twice he shied at a flutter of woman-garments, retreated to a respectable distance and reconnoitred with a fine air of indifference, to find that the flutter accompanied the movements of some girl for whom he cared not at all.

In his nostrils was the indefinable, unmistakable picnic odor—the odor of crushed grasses and damp leaf-mould stirred by the passing of many feet, the mingling of cheap perfumes and starched muslin and iced lemonade and sandwiches; in his ears the jumble of laughter and of holiday speech, the squealing of children in a mob around the swing, the protesting squeak of the ropes as they swung high, the snorting of horses tied just outside the enchanted ground. And through the tree-tops he could glimpse the range-land lying asleep in the hot sunlight, unchanged, uncaring, with the wild range-cattle feeding leisurely upon the slopes and lifting heads occasionally to snuff suspiciously the unwonted sounds and smells that drifted up to them on vagrant breezes.

He introduced Dill to four or five men whom he thought might be congenial, left him talking solemnly with a man who at some half-forgotten period had come from Michigan, and wandered aimlessly on through the grove.

Fellows there were in plenty whom he knew, but he passed them with a brief word or two. Truth to tell, for the most part they were otherwise occupied and had no time for him.

He loitered over to the swing, saw that the enthusiasts who were making so much noise were all youngsters under fifteen or so and that they hailed his coming with a joy tinged with self-interest. He rose to the bait of one dark-eyed miss who had her hair done in two braids crossed and tied close to her head with red-white-and-blue ribbon, and who smiled alluringly and somewhat toothlessly and remarked that she liked to go 'way, '*way* up till it most turned over, and that it didn't scare her a bit. He swung her almost into hysterics and straightway found himself exceedingly popular with other braided-and-tied young misses. Charming Billy never could tell afterward how long or how many he swung 'way, '*way* up; he knew that he pushed and pushed until his arms ached and the hair on his forehead became unpleasantly damp under his hat.

"That'll just about have to do yuh, kids," he rebelled suddenly and left them, anxiously patting his hair and generally resettling himself as he went. Once more in a dispirited fashion he threaded the crowd, which had grown somewhat larger, side-stepped a group which called after him, and went on down to the creek.

"I'm about the limit, I guess," he told himself irritably. "Why the dickens didn't I have the sense and nerve to ride over and ask her straight out if she was coming? I coulda drove her over, maybe—if she'd come with me. I coulda took the bay team and top-buggy, and done the thing right. I coulda—hell, there's a *heap* uh things I coulda done that would uh been a lot more wise than what I did do! Maybe she ain't coming at all, and—"

On the heels of that he saw a spring-wagon, come rattling down the trail across the creek. There were two seats full, and two parasols were bobbing seductively, and one of them was blue. "I'll bet a dollar that's them now," murmured Billy, and once more felt anxiously of his hair where it had gone limp under his hat. "Darned kids— they'd uh kept me there till I looked like I'd been wrassling calves half a day," went with the patting. He turned and went briskly through an empty and untrampled part of the grove to the place where the wagon would be most likely to stop. "I'm sure going to make good to-day or—" And a little farther—"What if it ain't *them*?"

Speedily he discovered that it was "them," and at the same time he discovered something else which pleased him not at all. Dressed with much care, so that even Billy must reluctantly own him good-looking enough, and riding so close to the blue parasol that his horse barely escaped grazing a wheel, was the Pilgrim. He glared at Billy in unfriendly fashion and would have shut him off completely from approach to the wagon; but a shining milk can, left carelessly by a bush, caught the eye of his horse, and after that the Pilgrim was very busy riding erratically in circles and trying to keep in touch with his saddle.

Billy, grown surprisingly bold, went straight to where the blue parasol was being closed with dainty deliberation. "A little more, and you'd have been late for dinner," he announced, smiling up at her, and held out his eager arms. Diplomacy, perhaps, should have urged him to assist the other lady first—but Billy Boyle was quite too direct to be diplomatic and besides, the other lady was on the opposite side from him.

Miss Bridger may have been surprised, and she may or may not have been pleased; Billy could only guess at her emotions—granting she felt any. But she smiled down at him and permitted the arms to receive her, and she also permitted—though with some hesitation—Billy to lead her straight away from the wagon and its occupants and from the gyrating Pilgrim to the deep delights of the grove.

"Mr. Walland is a good rider, don't you think?" murmured Miss Bridger, gazing over her shoulder.

"He's a bird," said Billy evenly, and was polite enough not to mention what kind of bird. He was wondering what on earth had brought those two together and why, after that night, Miss Bridger should be friendly with the Pilgrim; but of these things he said nothing, though he did find a good deal to say upon pleasanter subjects.

So far as any one knew, Charming Billy Boyle, while he had done many things, had never before walked boldly into a picnic crowd carrying a blue parasol as if it were a rifle and keeping step as best he might over the humps and hollows of the grove with a young woman. Many there were who turned and looked again—and these were the men who knew him best. As for Billy, his whole attitude was one of determination; he was not particularly lover-like—had he wanted to be, he would not have known how. He was resolved to make the most of his opportunities, because they were likely to be few and because he had an instinct that he should know the girl better—he had even dreamed foolishly, once or twice, of some day marrying her. But to clinch all, he had no notion of letting the Pilgrim offend her by his presence.

So he somehow got her wedged between two fat women at one of the tables, and stood behind and passed things impartially and ate ham sandwiches and other indigestibles during the intervals. He had the satisfaction of seeing the Pilgrim come within ten feet of them, hover there scowling for a minute or two and then retreat. "He ain't forgot the licking I gave him," thought Billy vaingloriously, and hid a smile in the delectable softness of a wedge of cake with some kind of creamy filling.

"*I* made that cake," announced Miss Bridger over her shoulder when she saw what he was eating. "Do you like it as well as—chicken stew?"

Whereupon Billy murmured incoherently and wished the two fat women ten miles away. He had not dared—he would never have dared—refer to that night, or mention chicken stew or prune pies or even dried apricots in her presence; but with her own hand she had brushed aside the veil of constraint that had hung between them.

"I wish I'd thought to bring a prune pie," he told her daringly, in his eagerness half strangling over a crumb of cake.

"Nobody wants prune pie at a picnic," declared one of the fat women sententiously. "You might as well bring fried bacon and done with it."

"Picnics," added the other and fatter woman, "iss for getting somet'ings t' eat yuh don'd haff every day at home." To point the moral she reached for a plate of fluted and iced molasses cakes.

"I *love* prune pies," asserted Miss Bridger, and laughed at the snorts which came from either side.

Billy felt himself four inches taller just then. "Give me stewed prairie-chicken," he stooped to murmur in her ear—or, to be exact, in the blue bow on her hat.

"Ach, you folks didn'd ought to come to a picnic!" grunted the fatter woman in disgust.

The two who had the secret between them laughed confidentially, and Miss Bridger even turned her head away around so that their eyes could meet and emphasize the joke.

Billy looked down at the big, blue bow and at the soft, blue ruffly stuff on her shoulders—stuff that was just thin enough so that one caught elusive suggestions of the soft, pinky flesh beneath—and wondered vaguely why he had never noticed the beating in his throat before—and what would happen if he reached around and tilted back her chin and—"Thunder! I guess I've sure got 'em, all right!"

he brought himself up angrily, and refrained from carrying the subject farther.

It was rumored that the dancing would shortly begin in the schoolhouse up the hill, and Billy realized suddenly with some compunction that he had forgotten all about Dill. "I want to introduce my new boss to yuh, Miss Bridger," he said when they had left the table and she was smoothing down the ruffly blue stuff in an adorably feminine way. "He isn't much just to look at, but he's the whitest man I ever knew. You wait here a minute and I'll go find him"—which was a foolish thing for him to do, as he afterward found out.

For when he had hunted the whole length of the grove, he found Dill standing like a blasted pine tree in the middle of a circle of men—men who were married, and so were not wholly taken up with the feminine element—and he was discoursing to them earnestly and grammatically upon the capitalistic tendencies of modern politics. Billy stood and listened long enough to see that there was no hope of weaning his interest immediately, and then went back to where he had left Miss Bridger. She was not there. He looked through the nearest groups, approached one of the fat women, who was industriously sorting the remains of the feast and depositing the largest and most attractive pieces of cake in her own basket, and made bold to inquire if she knew where Miss Bridger had gone.

"Gone home after some prune pie, I guess maybe," she retorted quellingly, and Billy asked no farther.

Later he caught sight of a blue flutter in the swing; investigated and saw that it was Miss Bridger, and that the Pilgrim, smiling and with his hat set jauntily back on his head, was pushing the swing. They did not catch sight of Billy for he did not linger there. He turned short around, walked purposefully out to the edge of the grove where his horse was feeding at the end of his rope, picked up the rope and led the horse over to where his saddle lay on its side, the neatly folded saddle-blanket laid across it. "Darn it, stand still!" he growled unjustly, when the horse merely took the liberty of switching a fly off his rump. Billy picked up the blanket, shook the wrinkles out mechanically, held it before him ready to lay across the waiting back of Barney; shook it again, hesitated and threw it violently back upon the saddle.

"Go on off—I don't want nothing of yuh," he admonished the horse, which turned and looked at him inquiringly. "I ain't through yet—I got another chip to put up." He made him a cigarette, lighted it and strolled nonchalantly back to the grove.

CHAPTER XI.
"When I Lift My Eyebrows This Way."

"Oh, where have you been, Billy boy, Billy boy?
Oh, where have you been, charming Billy?"
Somewhere behind him a daring young voice was singing. Billy turned with a real start, and when he saw her coming gayly down a little, brush-hidden path and knew that she was alone, the heart of him turned a complete somersault—from the feel of it.

"My long friend, Dilly, was busy, and so I—I went to look after my horse," he explained, his mind somewhat in a jumble. How came she to be there, and why did she sing those lines? How did she know that was *his* song, or—did she really care at all? And where was the Pilgrim?

"Mr. Walland and I tried the swing, but I don't like it; it made me horribly dizzy," she said, coming up to him. "Then I went to find Mama Joy—"

"Who?" Billy had by that time recovered his wits enough to know just exactly what she said.

"Mama Joy—my stepmother. I call her that. You see, father wants me to call her mama—he really wanted it mother, but I couldn't—and she's so young to have me for a daughter, so she wants me to call her Joy; that's her name. So I call her both and please them both, I hope. Did you ever study diplomacy, Mr. Boyle?"

"I never did, but I'm going to start right in," Billy told her, and half meant it.

"A thorough understanding of the subject is indispensable—when you have a stepmother—a *young* stepmother. You've met her, haven't you?"

"No," said Billy. He did not want to talk about her stepmother, but he hated to tell her so. "Er—yes, I believe I did see her once, come to think of it," he added honestly when memory prompted him.

Miss Bridger laughed, stopped, and laughed again. "How Mama Joy would *hate* you if she knew that!" she exclaimed relishfully.

"Why?"

"Oh, you wait! If ever I tell her that you—that *anybody* ever met her and then forgot! Why, she knows the color of your hair and eyes, and she knows the pattern of that horsehair hat-band and the size of your boots—she *admires* a man whose feet haven't two or three inches for every foot of his height—she says you wear fives, and you don't lack much of being six feet tall, and—"

"Oh, for Heaven's sake!" protested Billy, very red and uncomfortable. "What have I done to yuh that you throw it into me like that? My hands are up—and they'll stay up if you'll only quit it."

Miss Bridger looked at him sidelong and laughed to herself. "That's to pay you for forgetting that you ever met Mama Joy," she asserted. "I shouldn't be surprised if next week you'll have forgotten that you ever met *me*. And if you do, after that chicken stew—"

"You're a josher," said Billy helplessly, not being prepared to say just all he thought about the possibility of his forgetting her. He wished that he understood women better, so that he might the better cope with the vagaries of this one; and so great was his ignorance that he never dreamed that every man since Adam had wished the same thing quite as futilely.

"I'm not going to josh now," she promised, with a quick change of manner. "You haven't—I *know* you haven't, but I'll give you a chance to dissemble—you haven't a partner for the dance, have you?"

"No. Have you?" Billy did have the courage to say that, though he dared not say more.

"Well, I—I could be persuaded," she hinted shamelessly.

"Persuade nothing! Yuh belong to me, and if anybody tries to throw his loop over your head, why—" Billy looked dangerous; he meant the Pilgrim.

"Thank you." She seemed relieved, and it was plain she did not read into his words any meaning beyond the dance, though Billy was secretly hoping that she would. "Do you know, I think you're perfectly lovely. You're so—so *comfortable*. When I've known you a little longer I expect I'll be calling you Charming Billy, or else Billy Boy. If you'll stick close to me all through this dance and come every time I lift my eyebrows this way"—she came near getting kissed, right then, but she never knew it—"and say it's *your* dance and that I promised it to you before, I'll be—*awfully* grateful and obliged."

"I wisht," said Billy pensively, "I had the nerve to take all this for sudden admiration; but I savvy, all right. Some poor devil's going to get it handed to him to-night."

For the first time Miss Bridger blushed consciously. "I—well, you'll be good and obliging and do just what I want, won't you?"

"Sure!" said Billy, not trusting himself to say more. Indeed, he had to set his teeth hard on that word to keep more from tumbling out. Miss Bridger seemed all at once anxious over something.

"You waltz and two-step and polka and schottische, don't you?" Her eyes, as she looked up at him, reminded Billy achingly of that time in the line-camp when she asked him for a horse to ride home. They had the same wistful, pleading look. Billy gritted his teeth.

"Sure," he answered again.

Miss Bridger sighed contentedly. "I know it's horribly mean and selfish of me, but you're so good—and I'll make it up to you some time. Really I will! At some other dance you needn't dance with me once, or look at me, even—That will even things up, won't it?"

"Sure," said Billy for the third time.

They paced slowly, coming into view of the picnic crowd, hearing the incoherent murmur of many voices. Miss Bridger looked at him uncertainly, laughed a little and spoke impulsively. "You needn't do it, Mr. Boyle, unless you like. It's only a joke, anyway; I mean, my throwing myself at you like that. Just a foolish joke; I'm often foolish, you know. Of course, I know you wouldn't misunderstand or anything like that, but it *is* mean of me to drag you into it by the hair of the head, almost, just to play a joke on some one—on Mama Joy. You're too good-natured. You're a direct temptation to people who haven't any conscience. Really and truly, you needn't do it at all."

"Yuh haven't heard me raising any howl, have yuh?" inquired Billy, eying her slantwise. "I'm playing big luck, if yuh ask me."

"Well—if you *really* don't mind, and haven't any one else—"

"I haven't," Billy assured her unsmilingly. "And I really don't mind. I think I—kinda like the prospect." He was trying to match her mood and he was not at all sure that he was a success. "There's one thing. If yuh get tired uh having me under your feet all the time, why—Dilly's a stranger and an awful fine fellow; I'd like to have you— well, be kinda nice to him. I want him to have a good time, you see, and you'll like him. You can't help it. And it will square up anything yuh may feel yuh might owe me—"

"I'll be just lovely to Dilly," Miss Bridger promised him with emphasis. "It will be a fair bargain, then, and I won't feel so—so small about asking you what I did. You can help me play a little joke, and I'll dance with Duly. So," she finished in a tone of satisfaction, "we'll be even. I feel a great deal better now, because I can pay you back."

Billy, on that night, was more keenly observant than usual and there was much that he saw. He saw at once that Miss Bridger lifted her eyebrows in the way she had demonstrated as *this way*, whenever the Pilgrim approached her. He saw that the Pilgrim was looking extremely bloodthirsty and went out frequently—Billy guessed shrewdly that his steps led to where the drink was not water—and the sight cheered him considerably. Yet it hurt him a little to observe that, when the Pilgrim was absent or showed no sign of meaning to intrude upon her, Miss Bridger did not lift her eyebrows consciously. Still, she was at all times pleasant and friendly and he tried to be content.

"Mr. Boyle, you've been awfully good," she rewarded him when it was over. "And I think Mr. Dill is fine! Do you know, he waltzes beautifully. I'm sure it was easy to keep *my* side of the bargain."

Billy noticed the slight, inquiring emphasis upon the word *my*, and he smiled down reassuringly into her face. "Uh course mine was pretty hard," he teased, "but I hope I made good, all right."

"You," she said, looking steadily up at him, "are just exactly what I said you were. You are comfortable."

Billy did a good deal of thinking while he saddled Barney in the gray of the morning, with Dill at a little distance, looking taller than ever in the half light. When he gave the saddle its final, little tentative shake and pulled the stirrup around so that he could stick in his toe, he gave also a snort of dissatisfaction.

"Hell!" he said to himself. "I don't know as I care about being too *blame* comfortable. There's a limit to that kinda thing—with *her!*"

"What's that?" called Dill, who had heard his voice.

"Aw, nothing," lied Billy, swinging up. "I was just cussing my hoss."

CHAPTER XII.
Dilly Hires a Cook.

It is rather distressful when one cannot recount all sorts of exciting things as nicely fitted together as if they had been carefully planned and rehearsed beforehand. It would have been extremely gratifying and romantic if Charming Billy Boyle had dropped everything in the line of work and had ridden indefatigably the trail which led to Bridger's; it would have been exciting if he had sought out the Pilgrim and precipitated trouble and flying lead. But Billy, though he might have enjoyed it, did none of those things. He rode straight to the ranch with Dill—rather silent, to be sure, but bearing none of the marks of a lovelorn young man—drank three cups of strong coffee with four heaping teaspoonfuls of sugar to each cup, pulled off his boots, lay down upon the most convenient bed and slept until noon. When the smell of dinner assailed his nostrils he sat up yawning and a good deal tousled, drew on his boots and made him a cigarette. After that he ate his dinner with relish, saddled and rode away to where the round-up was camped, his manner utterly practical and lacking the faintest tinge of romance. As to his thoughts—he kept them jealously to himself.

He did not even glimpse Miss Bridger for three months or more. He was full of the affairs of the Double-Crank; riding in great haste to the ranch or to town, hurrying back to the round-up and working much as he used to work, except that now he gave commands instead of receiving them. For they were short-handed that summer and, as he explained to Dill, he couldn't afford to ride around and look as important as he felt.

"Yuh wait, Dilly, till we get things running the way I want 'em," he encouraged on one of his brief calls at the ranch. "I was kinda surprised to find things wasn't going as smooth as I used to think; when yuh haven't got the whole responsibility on your own shoulders, yuh don't realize what a lot of things need to be done. There's them corrals, for instance: I helped mend and fix and toggle 'em, but it never struck me how rotten they are till I looked 'em over this spring. There's about a million things to do before snow flies, or we won't be able to start out fresh in the spring with everything running smooth. And if I was you, Dilly, I'd go on a still hunt for another cook here at the ranch. This coffee's something fierce. I had my doubts about Sandy when we hired him. He always did look to me like he was built for herding sheep more than he was for cooking." This was in August.

"I have been thinking seriously of getting some one else in his place," Dill answered, in his quiet way. "There isn't very much to do here; if some one came who would take an interest and cook just what we wanted—I will own I have no taste for that peculiar mixture which Sandy calls 'Mulligan,' and I have frequently told him so. Yet he insists upon serving it twice a day. He says it uses up the scraps; but since it is never eaten, I cannot see wherein lies the economy."

"Well, I'd can him and hunt up a fresh one," Billy repeated emphatically, looking with disapproval into his cup.

"I will say that I have already taken steps toward getting one on whom I believe I can depend," said Dill, and turned the subject.

That was the only warning Billy had of what was to come. Indeed, there was nothing in the conversation to prepare him even in the slightest degree for what happened when he galloped up to the corral late one afternoon in October. It was the season of frosty mornings and of languorous, smoke-veiled afternoons, when summer has grown weary of resistance and winter is growing bolder in his advances, and the two have met in a passion-warmed embrace. Billy had ridden far with his riders and the trailing wagons, in the zest of his young responsibility sweeping the range to its farthest boundary of river or mountain. They were not through yet, but they had swung back within riding distance of the home ranch and Billy had come in for nearly a month's accumulation of mail and to see how Dill was getting on.

He was tired and dusty and hungry enough to eat the fringes off his chaps. He came to the ground without any spring to his muscles and walked stiffly to the stable door, leading his horse by the bridle reins. He meant to turn him loose in the stable, which was likely to be empty, and shut the door upon him until he himself had eaten something. The door was open and he went in unthinkingly, seeing nothing in the gloom. It was his horse which snorted and settled back on the reins and otherwise professed his reluctance to enter the place.

Charming Billy, as was consistent with his hunger and his weariness and the general mood of him, "cussed" rather fluently and jerked the horse forward a step or two before he saw some one poised hesitatingly upon the manger in the nearest stall.

"I guess he's afraid of *me*," ventured a voice that he felt to his toes. "I was hunting eggs. They lay them always in the awkwardest places to get at." She scrambled down and came toward him, bareheaded, with the sleeves of her blue-and-white striped dress rolled to her elbows— Flora Bridger, if you please.

Billy stood still and stared, trying to make the reality of her presence seem reasonable; and he failed utterly. His most coherent thought at that moment was a shamed remembrance of the way he had sworn at his horse.

Miss Bridger stood aside from the wild-eyed animal and smiled upon his master. "In the language of the range, 'come alive,' Mr. Boyle," she told him. "Say how-de-do and be nice about it, or I'll see that your coffee is muddy and your bread burned and your steak absolutely impregnable; because I'm here to *stay*, mind you. Mama Joy and I have possession of your kitchen, and so you'd better—"

"I'm just trying to let it soak into my brains," said Billy. "You're just about the last person on earth I'd expect to see here, hunting eggs like you had a right—"

"I *have* a right," she asserted. "Your Dilly—he's a perfect love, and I told him so—said I was to make myself

102

perfectly at home. So I have a perfect right to be here, and a perfect right to hunt eggs; and if I could make that sentence more 'perfect,' I would do it." She tilted her head to one side and challenged a laugh with her eyes.

Charming Billy relaxed a bit, yanked the horse into a stall and tied him fast. "Yuh might tell me how it happened that you're here," he hinted, looking at her over the saddle. He had apparently forgotten that he had intended leaving the horse saddled until he had rested and eaten—and truly it would be a shame to hurry from so unexpected a tête-à-tête.

Miss Bridger pulled a spear of blue-joint hay from a crack in the wall and began breaking it into tiny pieces. "It sounds funny, but Mr. Dill bought father out to get a cook. The way it was, father has been simply crazy to try his luck up in Klondyke; it's just like him to get the fever after everybody else has had it and recovered. When the whole country was wild to go he turned up his nose at the idea. And now, mind you, after one or two whom he knew came back with some gold, he must go and dig up a few million tons of it for himself! Your Dilly is rather bright, do you know? He met father and heard all about his complaint—how he'd go to the Klondyke in a minute if he could only get the ranch and Mama Joy and me off his hands—so what does Dilly do but buy the old ranch and hire Mama Joy and me to come here and keep house! Father, I am ashamed to say, was *abjectly* grateful to get rid of his incumbrances, and he—he hit the trail immediately." She stopped and searched absently with her fingers for another spear of hay.

"Do you know, Mr. Boyle, I think men are the most irresponsible creatures! A *woman* wouldn't turn her family over to a neighbor and go off like that for three or four years, just chasing a sunbeam. I—I'm horribly disappointed in father. A man has no right to a family when he puts everything else first in his mind. He'll be gone three or four years, and will spend all he has, and we—can shift for ourselves. He only left us a hundred dollars, to use in an emergency! He was afraid he might need the rest to buy out a claim or get machinery or something. So if we don't like it here we'll have to stay, anyway. We—we're 'up against it,' as you fellows say."

Charming Billy, fumbling the latigo absently, felt a sudden belligerence toward her father. "He ought to have his head punched good and plenty!" he blurted sympathetically.

To his amazement Miss Bridger drew herself up and started for the door. "I'm very sorry you don't like the idea of us being here, Mr. Boyle," she replied coldly, "but we happen to *be* here, and I'm afraid you'll just have to make the best of it!"

Billy was at that moment pulling off the saddle. By the time he had carried it from the stall, hung it upon its accustomed spike and hurried to the door, Miss Bridger was nowhere to be seen. He said "Hell!" under his breath, and took long steps to the house, but she did not appear to be there. It was "Mama Joy," yellow-haired, extremely blue-eyed, and full-figured, who made his coffee and gave him delicious things to eat—things which he failed properly to appreciate, because he ate with his ears perked to catch the faintest sound of another woman's steps and with his eyes turning constantly from door to window. He did not even know half the time what Mama Joy was saying, or see her dimples when she smiled; and Mama Joy was rather proud of her dimples and was not accustomed to having them overlooked.

He was too proud to ask, at supper time, where Miss Bridger was. She did not choose to give him sight of her, and so he talked and talked to Dill, and even to Mama Joy, hoping that Miss Bridger could hear him and know that he wasn't worrying a darned bit. He did not consider that he had said anything so terrible. What had she gone on like that about her father for, if she couldn't stand for any one siding in with her? Maybe he had put his sympathy a little too strong, but that is the way men handle each other. She ought to know he wasn't sorry she was there. Why, of *course* she knew that! The girl wasn't a fool, and she must know a fellow would be plumb tickled to have her around every day. Well, anyway, he wasn't going to begin by letting her lead him around by the nose, and he wasn't going to crumple down on his knees and tell her to please walk all over him.

"Well, anyway," he summed up at bedtime with a somewhat doubtful satisfaction, "I guess she's kinda got over the notion that I'm so blame *comfortable*—like I was an old grandpa-setting-in-the-corner. She's *got* to get over it, by thunder! I ain't got to that point yet; hell, no! I should say I hadn't!"

It is a fact that when he rode away just after sunrise next morning (he would have given much if duty and his pride had permitted him to linger a while) no one could have accused him of being in any degree a comfortable young man. For his last sight of Miss Bridger had been the flutter of her when she disappeared through the stable door.

CHAPTER XIII.
Billy Meets the Pilgrim.

The weeks that followed did not pass as quickly as before for Billy Boyle, nor did raking the range with his riders bring quite as keen a satisfaction with life. Always, when he rode apart in the soft haze and watched the sky-line shimmer and dance toward him and then retreat like a teasing maid, his thoughts wandered from the range and the cattle and the men who rode at his bidding and rested with one slim young woman who puzzled and tantalized him and caused him more mental discomfort than he had ever known in his life before that night when she entered so unexpectedly the line-camp and his life. He scarcely knew just how he did feel toward her; sometimes he hungered for her with every physical and mental fibre and was tempted to leave everything and go to her. Times there were when he resented deeply her treatment of him and repeated to himself the resolution not to lie down and let her walk all over him just because he liked her.

When the round-up was over and the last of the beef on the way to Chicago, and the fat Irish cook gathered up the reins of his four-horse team, mounted with a grunt to the high seat of the mess wagon and pointed his leaders thankfully into the trail which led to the Double-Crank, though the sky was a hard gray and the wind blew chill with the bite of winter and though tiny snowflakes drifted aimlessly to earth with a quite deceitful innocence, as if they knew nothing of more to come and were only idling through the air, the blood of Charming Billy rioted warmly through his veins and his voice had a lilt which it had long lacked and he sang again the pitifully foolish thing with which he was wont to voice his joy in living.

"I have been to see my wife,

She's the joy of my life,

She's a young thing, and cannot leave her mother!"

"Thought Bill had got too proud t' sing that song uh hisn," the cook yelled facetiously to the riders who were nearest. "I was lookin' for him to bust out in grand-opry, or something else that's a heap more stylish than his old come-all-ye."

Charming Billy turned and rested a hand briefly upon the cantle while he told the cook laughingly to go to the hot place, and then settled himself to the pace that matched the leaping blood of him. That pace soon discouraged the others and left them jogging leisurely a mile or two in the rear, and it also brought him the sooner to his destination.

"Wonder if she's mad yet," he asked himself, when he dismounted. No one seemed to be about, but he reflected that it was just about noon and they would probably be at dinner—and, besides, the weather was not the sort to invite one outdoors unless driven by necessity.

The smell of roast meat, coffee and some sort of pie assailed his nostrils pleasantly when he came to the house, and he went in eagerly by the door which would bring him directly to the dining room. As he had guessed, they were seated at the table. "Why, come in, William," Dill greeted, a welcoming note in his voice. "We weren't looking for you, but you are in good time. We've only just begun."

"How do you do, Mr. Boyle?" Miss Bridger added demurely.

"Hello, Bill! How're yuh coming?" cried another, and it was to him that the eyes of Billy Boyle turned bewilderedly. That the Pilgrim should be seated calmly at the Double-Crank table never once occurred to him. In his thoughts of Miss Bridger he had mentally eliminated the Pilgrim; for had she not been particular to show the Pilgrim that his presence was extremely undesirable, that night at the dance?

"Hello, folks!" he answered them all quietly, because there was nothing else that he could do until he had time to think. Miss Bridger had risen and was smiling at him in friendly fashion, exactly as if she had never run away from him and stayed away all the evening because she was angry.

"I'll fix you a place," she announced briskly. "Of course you're hungry. And if you want to wash off the dust of travel, there's plenty of warm water out here in the kitchen. I'll get you some."

She may not have meant that for an invitation, but Billy followed her into the kitchen and calmly shut the door behind him. She dipped warm water out of the reservoir for him and hung a fresh towel on the nail above the washstand in the corner, and seemed about to leave him again.

"Yuh mad yet?" asked Billy, because he wanted to keep her there.

"Mad? Why?" She opened her eyes at him. "Not as much as you look," she retorted then. "You look as cross as if—"

"What's the Pilgrim doing here?" Billy demanded suddenly and untactfully.

"Who? Mr. Walland?" She went into the pantry and came back with a plate for him. "Why, nothing; he's just visiting. It's Sunday, you know."

"Oh—is it?" Billy bent over the basin, hiding his face from her. "I didn't know; I'd kinda lost count uh the days." Whereupon he made a great splashing in his corner and let her go without more words, feeling more than ever that he needed time to think. "Just visiting—'cause it's *Sunday*, eh? The dickens it is!" Meditating deeply, he was very deliberate in combing his hair and settling his blue tie and shaking the dust out of his white silk neckerchief and retying it in a loose knot; so deliberate that Mama Joy was constrained to call out to him: "Your dinner is getting cold, Mr. Boyle," before he went in and took his seat where Miss Bridger had placed him—and he doubted much her innocence in the matter—elbow to elbow with the Pilgrim.

"How's shipping coming on, Billy?" inquired the Pilgrim easily, passing to him the platter of roast beef. "Most through, ain't yuh?"

"The outfit's on the way in," answered Billy, accepting noncommittally the meat and the overture for peace. "They'll be here in less than an hour."

If the Pilgrim wanted peace, he was thinking rapidly, what grounds had he for ignoring the truce? He himself had been the aggressor and he also had been the victor. According to the honor of fighting men, he should be generous. And when all was said and done—and the thought galled Billy more than he could understand—the offense of the Pilgrim had been extremely intangible; it had consisted almost wholly of looks and a tone or two, and he realized quite plainly that his own dislike of the Pilgrim had probably colored his judgment. Anyway, he had thrashed the Pilgrim and driven him away from camp and killed his dog. Wasn't that enough? And if the Pilgrim chose to forget the unpleasant circumstances of their parting and be friends, what could he do but forget also? Especially since the girl did not appear to be holding any grudge for what had passed between them in the line-camp. Billy, buttering a biscuit with much care, wished he knew just what *had* happened that night before he opened the door, and wondered if he dared ask her.

Under all his thoughts and through all he hated the Pilgrim, his bold blue eyes, his full, smiling lips and smooth cheeks, as he had never hated him before; and he hated himself because, being unable to account even to himself for his feelings toward the Pilgrim, he was obliged to hide his hate and be friends—or else act the fool. And above all the mental turmoil he was somehow talking and listening and laughing now and then, as if there were two of him and each one was occupied with his own affairs. "I wisht to thunder there was *three* uh me," he thought fleetingly during a pause. "I'd set the third one uh me to figuring out just where the girl stands in this game, and what she's thinking about right now. There's a kinda twinkling in her eyes, now and then when she looks over here, that sure don't line up with her innocent talk. I wisht I could mind-read her—

"Yes, we didn't get through none too soon. Looks a lot like we're going to get our first slice uh winter. We've been playing big luck that we didn't get it before now; and that last bunch uh beef was sure rollicky and hard to handle—we'd uh had a picnic with all the trimmings if a blizzard had caught us with them on our hands. As it is, we're all dead on our feet. I expect to sleep about four days without stopping for meals, if you ask *me*."

One cannot wonder that Charming Billy heard thankfully the clatter of his outfit arriving, or that he left half his piece of pie uneaten and hurried off, on the plea that he must show them what to do—which would have caused a snicker among the men if they had overheard him. He did not mind Dill following him out, nor did he greatly mind the Pilgrim remaining in the house with Miss Bridger. The relief of being even temporarily free from the perplexities of the situation mastered all else and sent him whistling down the path to the stables.

CHAPTER XIV.
A Winter at the Double-Crank.

There are times when, although the months as they pass seem full, nothing that has occurred serves to mark a step forward or back in the destiny of man. After a year, those months of petty detail might be wiped out entirely without changing the general trend of events—and such a time was the winter that saw "Dill and Bill," as one alliterative mind called them, in possession of the Double-Crank. The affairs of the ranch moved smoothly along toward a more systematic running than had been employed under Brown's ownership. Dill settled more and more into the new life, so that he was so longer looked upon as a foreign element; he could discuss practical ranch business and be sure of his ground—and it was then that Billy realized more fully how shrewd a brain lay behind those mild, melancholy blue eyes, and how much a part of the man was that integrity which could not stoop to small meanness or deceit. It would have been satisfying merely to know that such a man lived, and if Billy had needed any one to point the way to square living he must certainly have been better for the companionship of Dill.

As to Miss Bridger, he stood upon much the same footing with her as he had in the fall, except that he called her Flora, in the familiarity which comes of daily association; to his secret discomfort she had fulfilled her own prophecy and called him Billy Boy. Though he liked the familiarity, he emphatically did not like the mental attitude which permitted her to fall so easily into the habit of calling him that. Also, he was in two minds about the way she would come to the door of the living room and say: "Come, Billy Boy, and dry the dishes for me—that's a good kid!"

Billy had no objections to drying the dishes; of a truth, although that had been a duty which he shirked systematically in line-camps until everything in the cabin was in that state which compels action, he would have been willing to stand beside Flora Bridger at the sink and wipe dishes (and watch her bare, white arms, with the dimply elbows) from dark until dawn. What he did object to was the half-patronizing, wholly matter-of-fact tone of her, which seemed to preclude any possibility of sentiment so far as she was concerned. She always looked at him so frankly, with never a tinge of red in her cheeks to betray that consciousness of sex which goes ever—say what you like—with the love of a man and a maid.

He did not want her to call him "Billy Boy" in just that tone; it made him feel small and ineffective and young— he who was eight or nine years older than she! It put him down, so that he could not bring himself to making actual love to her—and once or twice when he had tried it, she took it as a great joke.

Still, it was good to have her there and to be friends. The absence of the Pilgrim, who had gone East quite suddenly soon after the round-up was over, and the generosity of the other fellows, who saw quite plainly how it was—with Billy, at least—and forbore making any advances on their own account, made the winter pass easily and left

Charming Billy in the spring not content, perhaps, but hopeful.

It was in the warm days of late April—the days which bring the birds and the tender, young grass, when the air is soft and all outdoors beckons one to come out and revel. On such a day Billy, stirred to an indefinable elation because the world as he saw it then was altogether good, crooned his pet song while he waited at the porch with Flora's horse and his own. They were going to ride together because it was Sunday and because, if the weather held to its past and present mood of sweet serenity, he might feel impelled to start the wagons out before the week was done; so that this might be their last Sunday ride for nobody knew how long.

"Let's ride up the creek," she suggested when she was in the saddle. "We haven't been up that way this spring. There's a trail, isn't there?"

"Sure, there's a trail—but I don't know what shape it's in. I haven't been over it myself for a month or so. We'll try it, but yuh won't find much to see; it's all level creek-bottom for miles and kinda monotonous to look at."

"Well, we'll go, anyway," she decided, and they turned their horses' heads toward the west.

They had gone perhaps five or six miles and were thinking of turning back, when Billy found cause to revise his statement that there was nothing to see. There had been nothing when he rode this way before, but now, when they turned to follow a bend in the creek and in the trail, they came upon a camp which looked more permanent than was usual in that country. A few men were lounging around in the sun, and there were scrapers of the wheeled variety, and wagons, and plows, and divers other implements of toil that were strange to the place. Also there was a long, reddish-yellow ridge branching out from the creek; Billy knew it for a ditch—but a ditch larger than he had seen for many a day. He did not say anything, even when Flora exclaimed over the surprise of finding a camp there, but headed straight for the camp.

When they came within speaking distance, a man showed in the opening of one of the tents, looked at them a moment, and came forward.

"Why, that's Fred Walland!" cried Flora, and then caught herself suddenly. "I didn't know he was back," she added, in a tone much less eager.

Billy gave her a quick look that might have told her much had she seen it. He did not much like the color which had flared into her cheeks at sight of the Pilgrim, and he liked still less the tone in which she spoke his name. It was not much, and he had the sense to push the little devil of jealousy out of sight behind him, but it had come and changed something in the heart of Billy.

"Why, hello!" greeted the Pilgrim, and Billy remembered keenly that the Pilgrim had spoken in just that way when he had opened the door of the line-camp upon them, that night. "I was going to ride over to the ranch, after a while. How are yuh, anyhow?" He came and held up his hand to Flora, and she put her own into it. Billy, with eyebrows pinched close, thought that they sure took their own time about letting go again, and that the smile which she gave the Pilgrim was quite superfluous to the occasion.

"Yuh seem to be some busy over here," he remarked carelessly, turning his eyes to the new ditch.

"Well, yes. Brown's having a ditch put in here. We only started a few days ago; them da—them no-account Swedes he got to do the rough work are so slow, we're liable to be at it all summer. How's everybody at the ranch? How's your mother, Miss Bridger? Has she got any mince pies baked?"

"I don't know—you might ride over with us and see," she invited, smiling at him again. "We were just going to turn back—weren't we, Billy Boy?"

"Sure!" he testified, and for the first time found some comfort in being called Billy Boy; because, if looks went for anything, it certainly made the Pilgrim very uncomfortable. The spirits of Billy rose a little.

"If you'll wait till I saddle up, I'll go along. I guess the Svenskies won't run off with the camp before I get back," said the Pilgrim, and so they stayed, and afterward rode back together quite amiably considering certain explosive elements in the party.

Perhaps Billy's mildness was due in a great measure to his preoccupation, which made him deaf at times to what the others were saying. He knew that they were quite impersonal in their talk, and so he drifted into certain other channels of thought.

Was Brown going to start another cow-outfit, or was he merely going to try his hand at farming? Billy knew that—

unless he had sold it—Brown owned a few hundred acres along the creek there; and as he rode over it now he observed the soil more closely than was his habit, and saw that, from a passing survey, it seemed fertile and free from either adobe or alkali. It must be that Brown was going to try ranching. Still, he had held out all his best stock, and Billy had not heard that he had sold it since. Now that he thought of it, he had not heard much about Brown since Dill bought the Double-Crank. Brown had been away, and, though he had known in a general way that the Pilgrim was still in his employ, he did not know in what capacity. In the absorption of his own affairs he had not given the matter any thought, though he had wondered at first what crazy impulse caused Brown to sell the Double-Crank. Even now he did not know, and when he thought of it the thing irritated him like a puzzle before it is solved.

So greatly did the matter trouble him that immediately upon reaching the ranch he left Flora and the Pilgrim and hunted up Dill. He found him hunched like a half-open jackknife in a cane rocker, with his legs crossed and one long, lean foot dangling loosely before him; he was reading "The Essays of Elia," and the melancholy of his face gave Billy the erroneous impression that the book was extremely sad, and caused him to dislike it without ever looking inside the dingy blue covers.

"Say, Dilly, old Brown's putting in a ditch big enough to carry the whole Missouri River. Did yuh know it?"

Dill carefully creased down the corner of the page where he was reading, untangled his legs and pulled himself up a bit in the chair. "Why, no, I don't think I have heard of it," he admitted. "If I have it must have slipped my mind—which isn't likely." Dill was rather proud of his capacity for keeping a mental grasp on things.

"Well, he's got a bunch uh men camped up the creek and the Pilgrim to close-herd 'em—and I'm busy wondering what he's going to do with that ditch. Brown don't do things just to amuse himself; yuh can gamble he aims to make that ditch pack dollars into his jeans—and if yuh can tell me *how*, I'll be a whole lot obliged." Dill shook his head, and Billy went on. "Did yuh happen to find out, when yuh was bargaining for the Double-Crank, how much land Brown's got held out?"

"No-o—I can't say I did. From certain remarks he made, I was under the impression that he owns quite a tract. I asked about getting all the land he had, and he said he preferred not to put a price on it, but that it would add considerably to the sum total. He said I would not need it, anyhow, as there is plenty of open range for the stock. He was holding it, he told me, for speculation and had never made any use of it in running his stock, except as they grazed upon it."

"Uh-huh. That don't sound to me like any forty-acre field; does it to you?"

"As I said," responded Dill, "I arrived at the conclusion that he owns a good deal of land."

"And I'll bet yuh the old skunk is going to start up a cow-outfit right under our noses—though why the dickens the Double-Crank wasn't good enough for him gets me."

"If he does," Dill observed calmly, "the man has a perfect right to do so, William. We must guard against that greed which would crowd out every one but ourselves—like pigs around a trough of sour milk! I will own, however—"

"Say, Dilly! On the dead, are yuh religious?"

"No, William, I am not, in the sense you mean. I hope, however, that I am honest. If Mr. Brown intends to raise cattle again I shall be glad to see him succeed."

Charming Billy sat down suddenly, as though his legs would no longer support him, and looked queerly at Dill.

"Hell!" he said meditatively, and sought with his fingers for his smoking material.

Dill showed symptoms of going back to "The Essays of Elia," so that Billy was stirred to speech.

"Now, looky here, Dilly. You're all right, as far as yuh go—but this range is carrying just about all the stock it needs right at present. I don't reckon yuh realize that all the good bottoms and big coulées are getting filled up with nesters; one here and one there, and every year a few more. It ain't much, uh course, but every man that comes is cutting down the range just that much. And I know one thing: when Brown had this outfit himself he was mighty jealous uh the range, and he didn't take none to the idea of anybody else shoving stock onto it more than naturally drifted on in the course uh the season. If he's going to start another cow-outfit, I'll bet yuh he's going to gobble land—and that's what *we* better do, and do it sudden."

"Since I have never had much personal experience in the 'gobbling' line, I'm afraid you'll have to explain," said Dill dryly.

"I mean leasing. We got to beat Brown to it. We got to start in and lease up all the land we can get our claws on. I ain't none desirable uh trying to make yuh a millionaire, Dilly, whilst we've only got one lone section uh land and about twelve thousand head uh stock, and somebody else aiming to throw a big lot uh cattle onto our range. I kinda shy at any contract the size uh that one. I've got to start the wagons out, if this weather holds good, and I want to go with 'em—for a while, anyhow—and see how things stack up on the range. And what *you've* got to do is to go and lease every foot uh land you can. Eh? State land. All the land around here almost is State land—all that's surveyed and that ain't held by private owners. And State land can be leased for a term uh years.

"The way they do it, yuh start in and go over the map all samee flea; yuh lease a section here and there and skip one and take the next, and so on, and then if yuh need to yuh throw a fence around the whole blame chunk—and there yuh are. No, it *ain't* cheating, because if anybody don't like it real bad, they can raise the long howl and make yuh revise your fencing; but in this neck uh the woods folks don't howl over a little thing like that, because you could lift up your own voice over something they've done, and there'd be a fine, pretty chorus! So that's what yuh can do if yuh want to—but anyway, yuh want to get right after that leasing. It'll cost yuh something, but we're just plumb obliged to protect ourselves. See?"

At that point he heard Flora laugh, and got up hastily, remembering the presence of the Pilgrim on the ranch.

"I see, and I will think it over and take what precautionary measures are necessary and possible."

Billy, not quite sure that he had sufficiently impressed Dill with the importance of the matter, turned at the door and looked in again, meaning to add an emphatic word or two; but when he saw that Dill was staring round-eyed at nothing at all, and that Lamb was lying sprawled wide open on the floor, his face relaxed from its anxious determination.

"I got his think-works going—he'll do the rest," he told himself satisfiedly, and pushed the subject from him. Just now he wanted to make sure the Pilgrim wasn't getting more smiles than were coming to him—and if you had left the decision of that with Billy, the Pilgrim would have had none at all.

"I wisht he'd *do* something I could lay my finger on—damn him," he reflected. "I can't kick him out on the strength uh my own private opinion. I'd just simply lay myself wide open to all kinds uh remarks. I *ain't* jealous; he ain't got any particular stand-in with Flora—but if I started action on him, that's what the general verdict would be. Oh, thunder!"

Nothing of his thoughts showed in his manner when he went out to where they were. He found them just putting up a target made of a sheet of tablet paper marked with a lead pencil into rings and an uncertain centre, and he went straight into the game with a smile. He loaded the gun for Flora, showed her exactly how to "draw a fine bead," and otherwise deported himself in a way not calculated to be pleasing to the Pilgrim. He called her Flora boldly whenever occasion offered, and he exulted inwardly at the proprietary way in which she said "Billy Boy" and ordered him around. Of course, *he* knew quite well that there was nothing but frank-eyed friendship back of it all; but the Pilgrim plainly did not know and was a good deal inclined to sulk over his interpretation.

So Billy, when came the time for sleeping, grinned in the dark of his room and dwelt with much satisfaction upon the manner of the Pilgrim's departure. He prophesied optimistically that he guessed that would hold the Pilgrim for a while, and that he himself could go on round-up and not worry any over what was happening at the ranch.

For the Pilgrim had come into the kitchen, ostensibly for a drink of water, and had found Miss Flora fussily adjusting the Klondyke nugget pin in the tie of Charming Billy, as is the way of women when they know they may bully a man with impunity—and she was saying: "Now, Billy Boy, if you don't learn to stick that pin in straight and not have the point standing out a foot, I'll—" That is where the Pilgrim came in and interrupted. And he choked over the dipper of water even as Billy choked over his glee, and left the ranch within fifteen minutes and rode, as Billy observed to the girl, "with a haughty spine."

"Oh, joy!" chuckled Billy when he lived those minutes over again, and punched the pillow facetiously. "Oh, joy, oh Johnathan! I guess maybe he didn't get a jolt, huh? And the way—the very *tone* when I called her Flora—sounded like the day was set for the wedding and we'd gone and ordered the furniture!"

The mood of him was still triumphant three days after when he turned in his saddle and waved his hand to Flora, who waved wistfully back at him. "It ain't any cinch right now—but I'll have her yet," he cheered himself when the twinge of parting was keenest.

CHAPTER XV.
The Shadow Falls Lightly.

Over the green uplands, into the coulées and the brushy creek-bottoms swept the sun-browned riders of the Double-Crank; jangling and rattling over untrailed prairie sod, the bed and mess wagons followed after with hasty camping at the places Billy appointed for brief sleeping and briefer eating, a hastier repacking and then the hurry over the prairies to the next stop. Here, a wide coulée lay yawning languorously in the sunshine with a gossipy trout stream for company; with meadowlarks rippling melodiously from bush and weed or hunting worms and bugs for their nestful of gaping mouths; with gophers trailing snakily through the tall grasses; and out in the barren centre where the yellow earth was pimpled with little mounds, plump-bodied prairie dogs sitting pertly upon their stubby tails the while they chittered shrewishly at the world; and over all a lazy, smiling sky with clouds always drifting and trailing shadows across the prairie-dog towns and the coulée and the creek, and a soft wind stirring the grasses.

Then the prairie dogs would stand a-tiptoe to listen. The meadowlarks would stop their singing—even the trailing shadows would seem to waver uncertainly—and only the creek would go gurgling on, uncaring. Around a bend would rattle the wagons of the Double-Crank, with a lone rider trotting before to point the way; down to the very bank of the uncaring creek they would go. There would be hurrying to and fro with much clamor of wood-chopping, tent-raising and all the little man-made noises of camp life and cooking. There would be the added clamor of the cavvy, and later, of tired riders galloping heavily into the coulée, and of many voices upraised in full-toned talk with now and then a burst of laughter.

All these things, and the prairie folk huddled trembling in their homes, a mute agony of fear racking their small bodies. Only the creek and the lazy, wide-mouthed coulee and the trailing clouds and the soft wind seemed not to mind.

Came another sunrise and with it the clamor, the voices, the rattle of riding gear, the trampling. Then a final burst and rattle, a dying of sounds in the distance, a silence as the round-up swept on over the range-land, miles away to the next camping place. Then the little prairie folk—the gopher, the plump-bodied prairie dogs, the mice and the rabbits, would listen long before they crept timidly out to sniff suspiciously the still-tainted air and inspect curiously and with instinctive aversion the strange marks left on the earth to show that it was all something more than a horrible nightmare.

So, under cloud and sun, when the wind blew soft and when it raved over the shrinking land, when the cold rain drove men into their yellow slickers and set horses to humping backs and turning tail to the drive of it and one heard the cook muttering profanity because the wood was wet and the water ran down the stovepipe and hungry men must wait because the stove would not "draw," the

Double-Crank raked the range. Horses grew lean and ill-fitting saddles worked their wicked will upon backs that shrank to their touch of a morning. Wild range cattle were herded, a scared bunch of restlessness, during long, hot forenoons, or longer, hotter afternoons, while calves that had known no misfortune beyond a wet back or a searching wind learned, panic-stricken, the agony of capture and rough handling and tight-drawn ropes and, last and worst, the terrible, searing iron.

There were not so many of them—these reluctant, wild-eyed pupils in the school of life. Charming Billy, sitting his horse and keeping tally of the victims in his shabby little book, began to know the sinking of spirit that comes to a man when he finds that things have, after all, gone less smoothly than he had imagined. There were withered carcasses scattered through the coulée bottoms and upon side hills that had some time made slippery climbing for a poor, weak cow. The loss was not crippling, but it was greater than he had expected. He remembered certain biting storms which had hidden deep the grasses, and certain short-lived chinooks that had served only to soften the surface of the snow so that the cold, coming after, might freeze it the harder.

It had not been a hard winter, as winters go, but the loss of cows had been above the average and the crop of calves below, and Billy for the first time faced squarely the fact that, in the cattle business as well as in others, there are downs to match the ups. In his castle building, and so far in his realization of his dreams, he had not taken much account of the downs.

Thus it was that, when they swung back from the reservation and camped for a day upon lower Burnt Willow, he felt a great yearning for the ranch and for sight of the girl who lived there. For excuses he had the mail and the natural wish to consult with Dill, so that, when he saddled Barney and told Jim Bleeker to keep things moving till to-morrow or the day after, he had the comfortable inner assurance that there were no side-glances or smiles and no lowered lids when he rode away. For Charming Billy, while he would have faced the ridicule of a nation if that were the price he must pay to win his deep desire, was yet well pleased to go on his way unwatched and unneeded.

Since the Double-Crank ranch lay with Burnt Willow Creek loitering through the willows within easy gunshot of the corrals, Billy's trail followed the creek except in its most irresponsible windings, when he would simplify his journey by taking straight as might be across the prairie. It was after he had done this for the second time and had come down to the creek through a narrow, yellow-clay coulee that he came out quite suddenly upon a thing he had not before seen.

Across the creek, which at that point was so narrow that a horse could all but clear it in a running jump, lay the hills, a far-reaching ocean of fertile green. Good grazing it was, as Billy well knew. In another day the Double-Crank riders would be sweeping over it, gathering the cattle; at least, that had been his intent. He looked across and his eyes settled immediately upon a long, dotted line drawn straight away to the south; at the far end a tiny huddle of figures moved indeterminately, the details of their business blunted by the distance. But Charming Billy, though he liked them little, knew well when he looked upon a fence in the building. The dotted line he read for post holes and the distant figures for the diggers.

While his horse drank he eyed the line distrustfully until he remembered his parting advice to Dill. "Dilly's sure getting a move on him," he decided, estimating roughly the size of the tract which that fence, when completed, would inclose. To be sure, it was pure guesswork, for he was merely looking at one corner. Up the creek he could not see, save a quarter mile or so to the next bend; even that distance he could not see the dotted line—for he was looking upon a level clothed with rank weeds and grass and small brush—but he knew it must be there. When he turned his horse from the water and went his way, his mind was no longer given up to idle dreaming of love words and a girl. This fencing business concerned him intimately, and his brain was as alert as his eyes. For he had not meant that Dilly should fence any land just yet.

Farther up the creek he crossed, meaning to take another short cut and so avoid a long detour; also, he wanted to see just where and how far the fence went. Yes, the post holes were there, only here they held posts leaning loosely this way and that like drunken men. A half mile farther the wire was already strung, but not a man did he see whom he might question—and when he glanced and saw that the sun was almost straight over his head and that Barney's shadow scurried along nearly beneath his stirrup, he knew that they would be stopping for dinner. He climbed a hill and came plump upon a fence, wire-strung, wire-stayed, aggressively barring his way.

"Dilly's about the most thorough-minded man I ever met up with," he mused, half annoyed, stopping a moment to survey critically the barrier. "Yuh never find a job uh hisn left with any loose ends a-dangling. He's got a fence here like he was guarding a railroad right-uh-way. I guess I'll go round, this trip."

At the ranch Charming Billy took the path that led to the kitchen, because when he glanced that way from the stable he caught a flicker of pink—a shade of pink which he liked very much, because Flora had a dress of that color and it matched her cheeks, it seemed to him. She had evidently not seen him, and he thought he would surprise her. To that end, he suddenly stopped midway and removed his spurs lest their clanking betray him. So he went on, with his eyes alight and the blood of him jumping queerly.

Just outside the door he stopped, saw the pink flutter in the pantry and went across the kitchen on his toes; sure, he was going to surprise her a lot! Maybe, he thought daringly, he'd kiss her—if his nerve stayed with him long enough. He rather thought it would. She was stooping a little over the flour barrel, and her back was toward him.

More daring than he would have believed of himself, he reached out his arms and caught her to him, and—It was not Flora at all. It was Mama Joy.

"Oh, I—I beg your pardon—I—" stammered Billy helplessly.

"Billy! You're a bad boy; how you frightened me!" she gasped, and showed an unmistakable inclination to snuggle.

Charming Billy, looking far more frightened than she, pulled himself loose and backed away. Mama Joy looked at him, and there was that in her eyes which sent a qualm of something very like disgust over Billy, so that in his toes he felt the quiver.

"It was an accident, Mrs. Bridger," he said laconically, and went out hastily, leaving her standing there staring after him.

Outside, he twitched his shoulders as if he would still free himself of something distasteful. "Hell! What do I want with *her*?" he muttered indignantly, and did not stop to think where he was going until he brought up at the stable. He had the reins of Barney in his hand, and had put his foot in the stirrup before he quite came to himself. "Hell!" he exploded again, and led Barney back into the stall.

Charming Billy sat down on a box and began to build a smoke; his fingers shook a great deal, so that he sifted out twice as much tobacco as he needed. He felt utterly bewildered and ashamed and sorry, and he could not think very clearly. He lighted the cigarette, smoked it steadily, pinched out the stub and rolled another before he came back to anything like calm.

Even when he could bring himself to face what had happened and what it meant, he winced mentally away from the subject. He could still feel the clinging pressure of her round, bare arms against his neck, and he once more gave his shoulders a twitch. Three cigarettes he smoked, staring at a warped board in the stall partition opposite him.

When the third was burned down to a very short stub he pinched out the fire, dropped the stab to the dirt floor and deliberately set his foot upon it, grinding it into the damp soil. It was as if he also set his foot upon something else, so grimly intent was the look on his face.

"Hell!" he said for the third time, and drew a long breath. "Well, this has got to stop right here!" He got up, took off his hat and inspected it gravely, redimpled the crown, set it upon his head a trifle farther back than usual, stuck his hands aggressively into his pockets and went back to the house. This time he did not go to the kitchen but around to the front porch, and he whistled shrilly the air of his own pet ditty that his arrival might be heralded before him.

Later, when he was sitting at the table eating a hastily prepared dinner with Mama Joy hovering near and seeming, to the raw nerves of Billy, surrounded by an atmosphere of reproach and coy invitation, he kept his eyes turned from her and ate rapidly that he might the sooner quit her presence. Flora was out riding somewhere, she told him when he asked. Dill came in and saved Billy from fleeing the place before his hunger slept, and Billy felt justified in breathing easily and in looking elsewhere than at his plate.

"I see you've been getting busy with the barbwire," he remarked, when he rose from the table and led the way out to the porch.

"Why, no. I haven't done any fencing at all, William," Dill disclaimed.

"Yuh haven't? Who's been fencing up all Montana south uh the creek, then?" Billy turned, a cigarette paper fluttering in his fingers, and eyed Dill intently.

"I believe Mr. Brown is having some fencing done. Mr. Walland stopped here to-day and said they were going to turn in a few head of cattle as soon as the field was finished."

"The dickens they are!" Billy turned away and sought a patch of shade where he might sit on the edge of the porch and dig his heels into the soft dirt. He dug industriously while he turned the matter over in his mind, then looked up a bit anxiously at Dill.

"Say, Dilly, yuh fixed up that leasing business, didn't yuh?" he inquired. "How much did yuh get hold of?"

Dill, towering to the very eaves of the porch, gazed down solemnly upon the other. "I'm afraid you will think it bad news, William. I did not lease an acre. I went, and I tried, but I discovered that others had been there before me. As you would say, they beat me *to* it. Mr. Brown leased all the land obtainable, as long ago as last fall."

Billy did not even say a word. He merely snapped a match short off between his thumb and forefinger and ground the pieces into the dirt with his heel. Into the sunlight that had shone placidly upon the castle he had builded in the air for Dill and for himself—yes, and for one other—crept a shadow that for the moment dimmed the whole.

"Say, Dilly, it's hell when things happen yuh haven't been looking for and can't help," he said at last, smiling a little. "I'd plumb got my sights raised to having a big chunk uh Montana land under a Double-Crank lease, but I reckon they can come down a notch. We'll come out on top— don't yuh worry none about *that*."

"I'm not worrying at all, William. I did not expect to have everything come just as we wanted it; that, so far, has not been my experience in business—or in love." The last two words, if one might judge from the direction of his glance, were meant as pure sympathy.

Billy colored a little under the brown. "The calf-crop is running kinda short," he announced hurriedly. "A lot uh cows died off last winter, and I noticed a good many uh that young stock we shipped in laid 'em down. I was hoping we wouldn't have to take any more jolts this season—but maybe I've got more nerves than sense on this land business. I sure do hate to see old Brown cutting in the way he's doing—but if he just runs what cattle he can keep under fence, it won't hurt us none."

"He's fencing a large tract, William—a very large tract. It takes in—"

"Oh, let up, Dilly! I don't want to know how big it is—not right now. I'm willing to take my dose uh bad medicine when it's time for it—but I ain't none greedy about swallowing the whole bottle at once! I feel as if I'd got enough down me to do for a while."

"You are wiser than most people," Dill observed dryly.

"Oh, sure. Say, if I don't see Flora—I'm going to hike back to camp pretty quick—you tell her I'm going to try and pull in close enough to take in that dance at Hardup, the Fourth. I heard there was going to be one. We can't get through by then, and I may not show up at the ranch, but I'll sure be at the dance. I—I'm in a hurry, and I've got to go right now." Which he did, and his going savored strongly of flight.

Dill, looking after him queerly, turned and saw Mama Joy standing in the doorway. With eyes that betrayed her secret she, too, was looking after Billy.

"There is something more I wanted to say to William," explained Dill quite unnecessarily, and went striding down the path after him. When he reached the stable, however, he did not have anything in particular to say—or if he had, he refrained from disturbing Billy, who was stretched out upon a pile of hay in one of the stalls.

"My hoss ain't through eating, yet," said Billy, lifting his head like a turtle. "I'm going, pretty soon. I sure do love a pile uh fresh hay."

Their eyes met understandingly, and Dill shook his head.

"Too bad—too bad!" he said gravely.

CHAPTER XVI.
Self-defense.

The wagons of the Double-Crank had stopped to tarry over the Fourth at Fighting Wolf Spring, which bubbles from under a great rock in a narrow "draw" that runs itself out to a cherry-masked point halfway up the side of Fighting Wolf Butte. Billy, with wisdom born of much experience in the ways of a round-up crew when the Fourth of July draws near, started his riders at day-dawn to rake all Fighting Wolf on its southern side. "Better catch up your ridge-runners," he had cautioned, "because I'll set yuh plumb afoot if yuh don't." The boys, knowing well his meaning and that the circle that day would be a big one over rough country, saddled their best horses and settled themselves to a hard day's work.

Till near noon they rode, and branded after dinner to the tune of much scurrying and bawling and a great deal of dust and rank smoke, urged by the ever-present fear that they would not finish in time. But their leader was fully as anxious as they and had timed the work so that by four o'clock the herd was turned loose, the fires drenched with water and the branding irons put away.

At sundown the long slope from Fighting Wolf Spring was dotted for a space with men, fresh-shaven, clean-shirted and otherwise rehabilitated, galloping eagerly toward Hardup fifteen miles away. That they had been practically in the saddle since dawn was a trifle not to be considered; they would dance until another dawn to make up for it.

Hardup, decked meagrely in the colors that spell patriotism, was unwontedly alive and full of Fourth of July noises. But even with the distraction of a holiday and a dance just about to start and the surrounding country emptied of humans into the town, the clatter of the Double-Crank outfit—fifteen wiry young fellows hungry for play—brought men to the doors and into the streets.

Charming Billy, because his eagerness was spiced with expectancy, did not stop even for a drink, but made for the hotel. At the hotel he learned that his "crowd" was over at the hall, and there he hurried so soon as he had removed the dust and straightened his tie and brushed his hair and sworn at his upstanding scalp-lock, in the corner of the hotel office dedicated to public cleanliness.

It was a pity that such single-hearted effort must go unrewarded, but the fact remains that he reached the hall just as the couples were promenading for the first waltz. He was permitted the doubtful pleasure of a welcoming nod from Flora as she went by with the Pilgrim. Dill was on the floor with Mama Joy, and at a glance he saw how it was; the Pilgrim had "butted in" and come along with them. He supposed Flora really could not help it, but it was pretty hard lines, all the same. For even in the range-land are certain rules of etiquette which must be observed when men and women foregather in the pursuit of pleasure. Billy remembered ruefully how a girl must dance first, last, and oftenest with her partner of the evening, and must eat supper with him besides, whether she likes or not; to tweak this rule means to insult the man beyond forgiveness.

"Well, it wouldn't hurt me none if Flora *did* cut him off short," Billy concluded, his eyes following them resentfully whenever they whirled down to his end of the room. "The way I've got it framed up, I'd spoke for her first—if Dilly told her what I said."

Still, what he thought privately did not seem to have much effect upon realities. Flora he afterward saw intermittently while they danced a quadrille together, and she made it plain that she had not considered Billy as her partner; how could she, when he was trailing around over the country with the round-up, and nobody knew whether he would come or not? No, Mr. Walland did not come to the ranch so very often. She added naïvely that he was awfully busy. He had ridden in with them—and why not? Was there any reason—

Billy, though he could think of reasons in plenty, turned just then to balance on the corner and swing, and to do many other senseless things at the behest of the man on the platform, so that when they stood together again for a brief space, both were breathless and she was anxiously feeling her hair and taking out side combs and putting them back again, and Billy felt diffident about interrupting her and said no more about who was her partner.

An hour or so later he was looking about for her, meaning to dance with her again, when a man pushed him aside hurriedly and went across the floor and spoke angrily to another. Billy, moving aside so that he could see, discovered Flora standing up with the Pilgrim for the dance in another "set" that was forming. The man who had jostled him was speaking to them angrily, but Billy could not catch the words.

"He's drunk," called the Pilgrim to the floor manager. "Put him out!"

Several men left their places and rushed over to them. Because Flora was there and likely to be involved, Billy reached them first.

"This was *my* dance!" the fellow was expostulating. "She promised it to me."

"Aw, he's drunk," repeated the Pilgrim, turning to Billy. "It's Gus Svenstrom. He's got it in for me because I fired him last week. Throw him out! Miss Bridger isn't going to dance with a drunken stiff like him."

"Oh, I'll go—I ain't so drunk I've got to be carried!" retorted the other, and pushed his way angrily through the crowd.

Flora had kept her place. Though the color had gone from her cheeks, she seemed to have no intention of quitting the quadrille, so there was nothing for Billy to do but get off the floor and leave her to her partner. He went out after the Swede, and, seeing him headed for the saloon across from the hotel, followed aimlessly. He was not quite comfortable in the hall, anyway, for he had caught Mama Joy eying him strangely, and he thought she was wondering why he had not asked her to dance.

Charming Billy was not by nature a diplomat; it never once occurred to him that he would better treat Mama Joy as if that half minute in the kitchen had never been. He had said good evening to her when he first met her that evening, and he considered his duty done. He did not want to dance with her, and that was, in his opinion, an excellent reason for not doing so. He did not like to have her watching him with those big, round, blue eyes of hers, so he stayed in the saloon for a while and only left it to go to supper when some one said that the dance crowd was over there. There might be some chance that would permit him to eat with Flora.

There are moments in a town when, even with many people coming and going, one may look and see none. When Billy closed the door of the saloon behind him and started across to the hotel, not a man did he see, though there was sound in plenty from the saloons and the hotel and the hall. He was nearly half across the street when two men came into sight and met suddenly just outside a window of the hotel. Billy, in the gloom of starlight and no moon, could not tell who they were; he heard a sharp sentence or two, saw them close together, heard a blow. Then they broke apart and there was the flash of a shot. One man fell and the other whirled about as if he would run, but Billy was then almost upon them and the man turned back and stood looking down at the fallen figure.

"Damn him, he pulled a knife on me!" he cried defensively. Billy saw that it was the Pilgrim.

"Who is he?" he asked, and knelt beside the form. The man was lying just where the lamp-light streamed out from the window, but his face was in shadow. "Oh, it's that Swede," he added, and rose. "I'll get somebody; I believe he's dead." He left the Pilgrim standing there and hurried to the door of the hotel office.

In any other locality a shot would have brought on the run every man who heard it; but in a "cow-town," especially on a dance night, shots are as common as shouts. In Hardup that night there had been periodical outbursts which no one, not even the women, minded in the least.

So it was not until Billy opened the door, put his head in, and cried: "Come alive! A fellow's been shot, right out here," that there was a stampede for the door.

The Pilgrim still stood beside the other, waiting. Three or four stooped over the man on the ground. Billy was one of them.

"He pulled a gun on me," explained the Pilgrim. "I was trying to take it away from him, and it went off."

Billy stood up, and, as he did so, his foot struck against a revolver lying beside the Swede. He looked at the Pilgrim queerly, but he did not say anything. They were lifting the Swede to carry him into the office; they knew that he was dead, even before they got him into the light.

"Somebody better get word to the coroner," said the Pilgrim, fighting for self-control. "It was self-defense. My God, boys, I couldn't help it! He pulled a gun on me. Yuh saw it on the ground there, right where he dropped it."

Billy turned clear around and looked again at the Pilgrim, and the Pilgrim met his eyes defiantly before he turned away.

"I understood yuh to say it was a knife," he remarked slowly.

The Pilgrim swung back again. "I didn't—or, if I did, I was rattled. It was a gun—that gun on the ground. He met me there and started a row and said he'd fix me. He pulled his gun, and I made a grab for it and it went off. That's all there is to it." He stared hard at Billy.

There was much talk among the men, and several told how they had heard the Swede "cussing" Walland in the saloon that evening. Some remembered threats—the threats which a man will foolishly make when he is pouring whisky down his throat by the glassful. No one seemed to blame Walland in the least, and Billy felt that the Pilgrim was in a fair way to become something of a hero. It is not every man who has the nerve to grab a gun with which he is threatened.

They made a cursory search of the Pilgrim and found that he was not armed, and he was given to understand that he would be expected to stay around town until the coroner came and "sat" on the case. But he was treated to drinks right and left, and when Billy went to find Flora the Pilgrim was leaning heavily upon the bar with a glass in his hand and his hat far back on his head, declaiming to the crowd that he was perfectly harmless so long as he was left alone. But he wasn't safe to monkey with, and any man who came at him hunting trouble would sure get all he wanted and then some. He said he didn't kill people if he could help it—but a man was plumb obliged to, sometimes.

"I'm sure surprised to think I got off with m' life, last winter, when I hazed him away from line-camp; I guess I must uh had a close call, all right!" Billy snorted contemptuously and shut the door upon the wordy revelation of the Pilgrim's deep inner nature which had been until that night carefully hidden from an admiring world.

The dance stopped abruptly with the killing; people were already going home. Billy, with the excuse that he would be wanted at the inquest, hunted up Jim Bleeker, gave him charge of the round-up for a few days, and told him what route to take. For himself, he meant to ride home with Flora or know the reason why.

"Come along, Dilly, and let's get out uh town," he urged, when he had found him. "It's a kinda small burg, and at the rate the Pilgrim is swelling up over what he done, there won't be room for nobody but him in another hour. He's making me plumb nervous and afraid to be around him, he's so fatal."

"We'll go at once, William. Walland is drinking a great deal more than he should, but I don't think he means to be boastful over so unfortunate an affair. Do you think you are taking an altogether unprejudiced view of the matter? Our judgment," he added deprecatingly, "is so apt to be warped by our likes and dislikes."

"Well, if that was the case here," Billy told him shortly, "I've got dislike enough for him to wind my judgment up like a clock spring. I'll go see if Flora and her mother are ready." In that way he avoided discussing the Pilgrim, for Dill was not so dull that he failed to take the hint.

CHAPTER XVII.
The Shadow Darkens.

The inquest resulted to the satisfaction of those who wished well to the Pilgrim, for it cleared him of all responsibility for the killing. Gus Svenstrom had been drunk; he had been heard to make threats; he had been the aggressor in the trouble at the dance; and the Pilgrim, in the search men had made immediately after the shooting, had been found unarmed. The case was very plainly one of self-defense.

Billy, when questioned, repeated the Pilgrim's first words to him—that the Swede had pulled a knife; and told the jury, on further questioning, that he had not seen any gun on the ground until after he had gone for help.

Walland explained satisfactorily to the jury. He may have said knife instead of gun. He had heard some one say that the Swede carried a knife, and he had been expecting him to draw one. He was rattled at first and hardly knew what he did say. He did not remember saying it was a knife, but it was possible that he had done so. As to Billy's not seeing any gun at first—they did not question the Pilgrim about that, because Billy in his haste and excitement could so easily overlook an object on the ground. They gave a verdict of self-defense without any discussion, and the Pilgrim continued to be something of a hero among his fellows.

Billy, as soon as the thing was over, mounted in not quite the best humor and rode away to join his wagons. He had not ridden to the Double-Crank to hear Flora talk incessantly of Mr. Walland, and repeat many times the assertion that she did not see how, under the circumstances, he could avoid killing the man. Nor had he gone to watch Mama Joy dimple and frown by turns and give him sidelong glances which made him turn his head quickly away. He hated to admit to himself how well he understood her. He did not want to be rude, but he had no desire to flirt with her, and it made him rage inwardly to realize how young and pretty she really was, and how, if it were not for Flora, he might so easily be tempted to meet her at least halfway. She could not be more than four or five years older than Flora, and in her large, blonde way she was quite as alluring. Billy wished profanely that she had gone to Klondyke with her husband, or that Bridger had known enough about women to stay at home with a wife as young as she.

He was glad in his heart when came the time to go. Maybe she would get over her foolishness by the time he came in with the round-up. At any rate, the combination at the ranch did not tempt him to neglect his business, and he galloped down the trail without so much as looking back to see if Flora would wave—possibly because he was afraid he might catch the flutter of a handkerchief in fingers other than hers.

It was when the round-up was on its way in that Billy, stopping for an hour in Hardup, met Dill in the post office. "Why, hello, Dilly!" he cried, really glad to see the tall, lank form come shambling in at the door. "I didn't expect to see yuh off your own ranch. Anybody dead?" It struck him that Dill looked a shade more melancholy than was usual, even for him.

"Why, no, William. Every one is well—very well indeed. I only rode in after the mail and a few other things. I'm always anxious for my papers and magazines, you know. If you will wait for half an hour—you are going home, I take it?"

"That's where I'm sure headed, and we can ride out together, easy as not. We're through for a couple uh weeks or so, and I'm hazing the boys home to bust a few hosses before we strike out again. I guess I'll just keep the camp running down by the creek. Going to be in town long enough for me to play a game uh pool?"

"I was going right out again, but there's no particular hurry," said Dill, looking over his letters. "Were you going to play with some one in particular?"

"No—just the first gazabo I could rope and lead up to the table," Billy told him, sliding off the counter where he had been perched.

"I wouldn't mind a game myself," Dill observed, in his hesitating way.

In the end, however, they gave up the idea and started for home; because two men were already playing at the only table in Hardup, and they were in no mind to wait indefinitely.

Outside the town, Dill turned gravely to the other, "Did you say you were intending to camp down by the creek, William?" he asked slowly.

"Why, yes. Anything against it?" Billy's eyes opened a bit wider that Dill should question so trivial a thing.

"Oh, no—nothing at all." Dill cleared his throat raspingly. "Nothing at all—so long as there is any creek to camp beside."

"I reckon you've got something to back that remark. Has the creek went and run off somewhere?" Billy said, after a minute of staring.

"William, I have been feeling extremely ill at ease for the past week, and I have been very anxious for a talk with you. Eight days ago the creek suddenly ran dry—so dry that one could not fill a tin dipper except in the holes. I observed it about noon, when I led my horse down to water. I immediately saddled him and rode up the creek to discover the cause." He stopped and looked at Billy steadily.

"Well, I reckon yuh found it," Billy prompted impatiently.

"I did. I followed the creek until I came to the ditch Mr. Brown has been digging. I found that he had it finished and was filling it from the creek in order to test it. I believe," he added dryly, "he found the result very satisfying—to himself. The ditch carried the whole creek without any trouble, and there was plenty of room at the top for more!"

"Hell!" said Billy, just as Dill knew he would say. "But he can't take out any more than his water-right calls for," he added. "Yuh got a water right along with the ranch, didn't yuh say?"

"I got three—the third, fourth, and fifth. I have looked into the matter very closely in the last week. I find that we can have all the water there is—after Brown gets through. His rights are the first and second, and will cover all the water the creek will carry, if he chooses to use them to the limit. I suspect he was looking for some sort of protest from me, for he had the papers in his pocket and showed them to me. I afterward investigated, as I said, and found the case to be exactly as I have stated."

Billy stared long at his horse's ears. "Well, he can't use the whole creek," he said at last, "not unless he just turned it loose to be mean, and I don't believe he can waste water even if he does hold the rights. We can mighty quick put a stop to that. Do yuh know anything about injunctions? If yuh don't, yuh better investigate 'em a lot—because I don't know a damn' thing about the breed, and we're liable to need 'em bad."

"I believe I may truthfully say that I understand the uses—and misuses—of injunctions, William. In the East they largely take the place of guns as fighting weapons, and I think I may say without boasting that I can hit the bull's-eye with them as well as most men. But suppose Mr. Brown *uses* the water? Suppose there is none left to turn back into the creek channel when he is through? He has a large force of men at work running laterals from the main ditch, which carries the water up and over the high land, and I took the liberty of following his lines of stakes. As you would put it, William, he seems about to irrigate the whole of northern Montana; certainly his stakes cover the whole creek bottom, both above and below the main ditch, and also the bench land above."

"Hell! Anything else?"

"I believe not—except that he has completed his fencing and has turned in a large number of cattle. I say completed, though strictly speaking he has not. He has completed the great field south of the creek and east of us. But Mr. Walland was saying that Brown intends to fence a tract to the north of us, either this fall or early in the spring. I know to a certainty that he has a good many sections leased there. I tried to obtain some of it last spring and could not." Into the voice of Dill had crept a note of discouragement.

"Well, don't yuh worry none, Dilly. I'm here to see yuh pull out on top, and you'll do it, too. You're a crackerjack when it comes to the fine points uh business, and I sure savvy the range end uh the game, so between us we ought to make good, don't yuh think? You just keep your eye on Brown, and if yuh can slap him in the face with an injunction or anything, don't yuh get a sudden attack uh politeness and let him slide. I'll look after the cow brutes myself—and if I ain't good for it, after all these years, I ought to be kicked plumb off the earth. The time has gone by when we could ride over there and haze his bunch clear out uh the country on a high lope, with our six guns backing our argument. I kinda wish," he added pensively, "we *hadn't* got so damn' decent and law-abiding. We could get action a heap more speedy and thorough with a dozen or fifteen buckaroos that liked to fight and had lots uh shells and good hosses. Why, I could have the old man's bunch shoveling dirt into that ditch to beat four aces, in about fifteen minutes, if—"

"But, as you say," Dill cut in anxiously, "we are decent and law-abiding, and such a procedure is quite out of the question."

"Aw, I ain't meditating no moonlight attack, Dilly—but the boys would sure love to do it if I told 'em to get busy, and I reckon we could make a better job of it than forty-nine injunctions and all kinds uh law sharps."

"Careful, William. I used to be a 'law sharp' myself," protested Dill, pulling his face into a smile. "And I must own I feel anxious over this irrigation project of Brown's. He is going to work upon a large scale—a *very* large scale—for a private ranch. You have made it plain to me, William, how vitally important a wide, unsettled country is to successful cattle raising; and since then I have thought deeply upon the subject. I feel sure that Mr. Brown is *not* going to start a cattle ranch."

"If he ain't, then what—"

"I am not prepared at present to make a statement, even to you, William. I never enjoyed recanting. But one thing I may say. Mr. Brown has so far kept well within his legal rights, and we have no possible ground for protest. So you see, perhaps we would better turn our entire attention to our own affairs."

"Sure. I got plenty uh troubles uh my own," Billy agreed, more emphatically than he intended.

Dill looked at him hesitatingly. "Mrs. Bridger," he observed slowly, "has received news that her husband is seriously ill. There will not be another boat going north until spring, so that it will be impossible for her to go to him. I am extremely sorry." Then, as if that statement seemed to him too bald, in view of the fact that they had never discussed Mama Joy, he added, "It is very hard for Flora. The letter held out little hope of recovery."

Billy, though he turned a deep red and acquired three distinct creases between his eyebrows, did not even make use of his favorite expletive. After a while he said irritably that a man was a damn fool to go off like that and leave a wife—and family—behind him. He ought either to stay at home or take them with him.

He did not mean that he wished her father had taken Flora to Klondyke, though he openly implied that he wished Mama Joy had gone. He knew he was inconsistent, but he also knew—and there was comfort as well as discomfort in the knowledge—that Dill understood him very well.

It seemed to Billy, in the short time that the round-up crew was camped by the creek, that no situation could be more intolerable than the one he must endure. He could not see Flora without having Mama Joy present also—or if he did find Flora alone, Mama Joy was sure to appear very shortly. If he went near the house there was no escaping her. And when he once asked Flora to ride with him he straightway discovered that Mama Joy had developed a passion for riding and went along. Flora had only time to murmur a rapid sentence or two while Mama Joy was hunting her gloves.

"Mama Joy has been taking the *Ladies' Home Journal*" she said ironically, "and she has been converted to the idea that a girl must never be trusted alone with a man. I've acquired a chaperon now! Have you begun to study diplomacy yet, Billy Boy?"

"Does she chapyron yuh this fervent when the Pilgrim's the man?" countered Billy resentfully.

He did not get an answer, because Mama Joy found her gloves too soon, but he learned his lesson and did not ask Flora to ride with him again. Nevertheless, he tried surreptitiously to let her know the reason and so prevent any misunderstanding.

He knew that Flora was worrying over her father, and he would like to have cheered her all he could; but he had no desire to cheer Mama Joy as well—he would not even give her credit for needing cheer. So he stayed away from them both and gave his time wholly to the horse-breaking and to affairs in general, and ate and slept in camp to make his avoidance of the house complete.

Sometimes, of a night when he could not sleep, he wondered why it is that one never day-dreams unpleasant obstacles and disheartening failures into one's air castles. Why was it that, just when it had seemed to him that his dream was miraculously come true; when he found himself complete master of the Double-Crank where for years he had been merely one of the men; when the One Girl was also settled indefinitely in the household he called his home; when he knew she liked him, and had faith to believe he could win her to something better than friendship—all these good things should be enmeshed in a tangle of untoward circumstances?

Why must he be compelled to worry over the Double-Crank, that had always seemed to him a synonym for success? Why must his first and only love affair be hampered by an element so disturbing as Mama Joy? Why, when he had hazed the Pilgrim out of his sight—and as he supposed, out of his life—must the man hover always in the immediate background, threating the peace of mind of Billy, who only wanted to be left alone that he and his friends might live unmolested in the air castle of his building?

One night, just before they were to start out again gathering beef for the shipping season, Billy thought he had solved the problem—philosophically, if not satisfactorily. "I guess maybe it's just one uh the laws uh nature that you're always bumping into," he decided. "It's a lot like draw-poker. Yah can't get dealt out to yuh the cards yuh want, without getting some along with 'em that yuh don't want. What gets me is, I don't see how in thunder I'm going to ditch m' discard. If I could just turn 'em face down on the table and count 'em out uh the game—old Brown and his fences and his darn ditch, and that dimply blonde person and the Pilgrim—oh, hell! Wouldn't we rake in the stakes if I could?"

Straightway Billy found another element added to the list of disagreeables—or, to follow his simile, another card was dealt him which he would like to have discarded, but which he must keep in his hand and play with what skill he might. He was not the care-free Charming Billy Boyle who had made prune pie for Flora Bridger in the line-camp. He looked older, and there were chronic creases between his eyebrows, and it was seldom that he asked tunefully

"Can she make a punkin pie, Billy boy, Billy Boy?"

He had too much on his mind for singing anything.

It was when he had gathered the first train load of big, rollicky steers for market and was watching Jim Bleeker close the stockyard gate on the tail of the herd at Tower, the nearest shipping point, that the disagreeable element came in the person of Dill and the news he bore.

He rode up to where Billy, just inside the wing of the stockyards, was sitting slouched over with one foot out of the stirrup, making a cigarette. Dill did not look so much the tenderfoot, these days. He sat his horse with more assurance, and his face was brown and had that firm, hard look which outdoor living brings.

"I looked for you in yesterday or the day before, William," he said, when Billy had greeted him with a friendly, "Hello, Dilly!" and one of his illuminating smiles.

"I'm ready to gamble old Brown has been and gone and run the creek dry on yuh again," bantered Billy, determined at that moment to turn his back on trouble.

"No, William, you would lose. The creek is running almost its normal volume of water. I dislike very much to interfere with your part of the business, William, but under present conditions I feel justified in telling you that you must not ship these cattle just now. I have been watching the market with some uneasiness for a month. Beef has been declining steadily until now it ranges from two-ninety to three-sixty, and you will readily see, William, that we cannot afford to ship at that figure. For various reasons I have not obtruded business matters upon you, but I will now state that it is vitally important that we realize enough from the beef shipments to make our fall payment on the mortgage and pay the interest on the remainder. It would be a great advantage if we could also clear enough for the next year's running expenses. Have you any idea how much beef there will be to ship this fall?"

"I figured on sixty or seventy cars," said Billy. Instinctively he had pulled himself straight in the saddle to meet this fresh emergency.

Dill, with a pencil and an old letter from his pocket, was doing some rapid figuring. "With beef so low, I fear I shall be obliged to ask you to hold this herd for two or three weeks. The price is sure to rise later. It is merely a juggling operation among the speculators and is not justified by the condition of the stock, or of the market. In a couple of weeks the price should be normal again."

"And in a couple uh weeks this bunch would bring the lowest figure they name," Billy asserted firmly. "Beef shrinks on the hoof like thunder when it's held up and close-herded on poor range. What yuh better do, Dilly, is let me work this herd and ship just the top-notchers—they're *all* prime beef," he added regretfully, glancing through the fence at the milling herd. "I can cut out ten of twelve cars that'll bring top price, and throw the rest back on the range till we gather again. Yuh won't lose as much that way as yuh would by holding up the whole works."

"Well," Dill hesitated, "perhaps you are right. I don't pretend to know anything about this side of the business. To put the case to you plainly, we must clear forty thousand dollars on our beef this fall, for the mortgage alone—putting it in round numbers. We should also have ten thousand dollars for expenses, in order to run clear without adding to our liabilities. I rely upon you to help manage it. If you would postpone any more gathering of beef until—"

"It's just about a case uh now or never," Billy cut in. "There's only about so long to gather beef before they begin to fall off in weight. Then we've got to round up the calves and wean 'em, before cold weather sets in. We can't work much after snow falls. We can pull through the first storm, all right, but when winter sets in we're done. We've got to wean and feed all the calves you've got hay for, and I can save some loss by going careful and taking 'em away from the poorest cows and leaving the fat ones to winter their calves. How much hay yuh got put up?"

"A little over five hundred tons on our place," said Dill. "And I sent a small crew over to the Bridger place; they have nearly a hundred tons there. You said for me to gather every spear I could," he reminded humorously, "and I obeyed to the best of my ability."

"Good shot, Dilly. I'll round up eight or nine hundred calves, then; that'll help some. Well, shall I cut the top off this bunch uh beef, or throw the whole business back on the range? You're the doctor."

Dill rode close to the high fence, stood in his stirrups and looked down upon the mass of broad, sleek backs moving restlessly in and out and around, with no aim but to seek some way of escape. The bawling made speech difficult at any distance, and the dust sent him coughing away.

"I think, William," he said, when he was again beside Billy, "I shall leave this matter to your own judgment. What I want is to get every cent possible out of the beef we ship; the details I am content to leave with you, for in my ignorance I should probably botch the job. I suppose we can arrange it so that, in case the market rises suddenly, you can rush in a trainload at short notice?"

"Give me two weeks to get action on the range stuff, and I can have a trainload on the way to Chicago so quick it'll make your head whirl. I'll make it a point to be ready on short notice. And before we pull out I'll give yuh a kinda programme uh the next three or four weeks, so yuh can send a man out and he'll have some show uh finding us. And I won't bring in another herd till you send word—only yuh want to bear in mind that I can't set out there on a pinnacle till snow flies, waiting for prices to raise in Chicago. Yuh don't want to lose sight uh them nine hundred calves we've got to gather yet."

It was all well enough for Billy to promise largely and confidently, but he failed to take into account one small detail over which he had no control. So perfect was his system of gathering beef—and he gathered only the best, so as to catch the top price—that when Dill's message came, short and hurried but punctiliously worded and perfectly punctuated, that beef had raised to four-thirty and "Please rush shipment as per agreement," Billy had his trainload of beef in Tower, ready to load just three days after receiving notice. But here interfered the detail over which he had no control. Dill had remembered to order the cars, but shipping was heavy and cars were not to be had.

Two long, heartrending weeks they waited just outside Tower, held there within easy reach—and upon mighty short feed for the herd—by the promises of the railroad management and the daily assurance of the agent that the cars might be along at any time within four hours. (He always said four hours, which was the schedule time for fast freight between Tower and the division point.) Two long weeks, while from the surrounding hills they watched long stock trains winding snakily over the prairie toward Chicago. During those maddening days and nights Billy added a fresh crease to the group between his eyebrows and deepened the old ones, and Dill rode three horses thin galloping back and forth between the ranch and the herd, in helpless anxiety.

At last the cars came and the beef, a good deal thinner than it had been, was loaded and gone, and the two relaxed somewhat from the strain. The market was lower when that beef reached its destination, and they did not bring the "top" price which Billy had promised Dill.

So the shipping season passed and Dill made his payment on the mortgage by borrowing twelve thousand dollars, using a little over two thousand to make up the deficit in shipping returns and holding the remainder for current expenses. Truly, the disagreeable element which would creep in where Billy had least expected scored a point there, and once more the castle he had builded for himself and Dill and one other lay in shadow.

CHAPTER XVIII.
When the North Wind Blows.

November came in with a blizzard; one of those sudden, sweeping whirls of snow, with bitter cold and a wind that drove the fine snow-flour through shack walls and around window casings, and made one look speculatively at the supply of fuel. It was such a storm as brings an aftermath of sheepherders reported missing with their bands scattered and wandering aimlessly or else frozen, a huddled mass, in some washout; such a storm as sends the range cattle drifting, heads down and bodies hunched together, neither knowing nor caring where their trail may end, so they need not face that bitter drive of wind and snow.

It was the first storm of the season, and they told one another it would be the worst. The Double-Crank wagons were on the way in with a bunch of bawling calves and cows when it came, and they were forced to camp hastily in the shelter of a coulée till it was over, and to walk and lead their horses much of the time on guard that they might not freeze in the saddle. But they pulled through it, and they got to the ranch and the corrals with only a few calves left beside the trail to mark their bitter passing. In the first days of cold and calm that came after, the ranch was resonant day and night with that monotonous, indescribable sound, like nothing else on earth unless it be the beating of surf against a rocky shore—the bawling of nine hundred calves penned in corrals, their uproar but the nucleus for the protesting clamor of nine hundred cows circling outside or standing with noses pressed close against the corral rails.

Not one day and night it lasted, nor two. For four days the uproar showed no sign of ever lessening, and on the fifth the eighteen hundred voices were so hoarse that the calves merely whispered their plaint, gave over in disgust and began nosing the scattered piles of hay. The cows, urged by hunger, strayed from the blackened circle around the corrals and went to burrowing in the snow for the ripened grass whereby they must live throughout the winter. They were driven forth to the open range and left there, and the Double-Crank settled down to comparative quiet and what peace they might attain. Half the crew rolled their beds and rode elsewhere to spend the winter, returning, like the meadowlarks, with the first hint of soft skies and green grass.

Jim Bleeker and a fellow they called Spikes moved over to the Bridger place with as many calves as the hay there would feed, and two men were sent down to the line-camp to winter. Two were kept at the Double-Crank Ranch to feed the calves and make themselves generally useful—the quietest, best boys of the lot they were, because they must eat in the house and Billy was thoughtful of the women.

So the Double-Crank settled itself for the long winter and what it might bring of good or ill.

Billy was troubled over more things than one. He could not help seeing that Flora was worrying a great deal over her father, and that the relations between herself and Mama Joy were, to put it mildly and tritely, strained. With the shadow of what sorrow might be theirs, hidden away from them in the frost-prisoned North, there was no dancing to lighten the weeks as they passed, and the women of the range land are not greatly given to "visiting" in winter. The miles between ranches are too long and too cold and uncertain, so that nothing less alluring than a dance may draw them from home. Billy thought it a shame, and that Flora must be terribly lonesome.

It was a long time before he had more than five minutes at a stretch in which to talk privately with her. Then one morning he came in to breakfast and saw that the chair of Mama Joy was empty; and Flora, when he went into the kitchen afterward, told him with almost a relish in her tone that Mrs. Bridger—she called her that, also with a relish— was in bed with toothache.

"Her face is swollen on one side till she couldn't raise a dimple to save her life," she announced, glancing to see that the doors were discreetly closed. "It's such a relief, when you've had to look at them for four years. If *I* had dimples," she added, spitefully rattling a handful of knives and forks into the dishpan, "I'd plug the things with beeswax or dough, or anything that I could get my hands on. Heavens! How I hate them!"

"Same here," said Billy, with guilty fervor. It was treason to one of his few principles to speak disparagingly of a woman, but it was in this case a great relief. He had never before seen Flora in just this explosive state, and he had never heard her say "Heavens!" Somehow, it also seemed to him that he had never seen her so wholly lovable. He went up to her, tilted her head back a little, and put a kiss on the place where dimples were not. "That's one uh the reasons why I like yuh so much," he murmured. "Yuh haven't got dimples or yellow hair or blue eyes—thank the Lord! Some uh these days, girlie, I'm going t' pick yuh up and run off with yuh."

Her eyes, as she looked briefly up at him, were a shade less turbulent. "You'd better watch out or *she* will be running off with *you*!" she said, and drew gently away from him. "There! That's a horrid thing to say, Billy Boy, but it isn't half as horrid as—And she watches me and wants to know everything we say to each other, and is—" She stopped abruptly and turned to get hot water.

"I know it's tough, girlie." Charming Billy, considering his ignorance of women, showed an instinct for just the sympathy she needed. "I haven't had a chance to speak to yuh, hardly, for months—anything but common remarks made in public. How long does the toothache last as a general thing?" He took down the dish towel from its nail inside the pantry door and prepared to help her. "She's good for to-day, ain't she?"

"Oh, yes—and I suppose it *does* hurt, and I ought to be sorry. But I'm not. I'm glad of it. I wish her face would stay that way all winter! She's so fussy about her looks she won't put her nose out of her room till she's pretty again. Oh, Billy Boy, I wish I were a man!"

"Well, *I* don't!" Billy disagreed. "If yuh was," he added soberly, "and stayed as pretty as yuh are now, she'd—" But Billy could not bring himself to finish the sentence.

"Do you think it's because you're so pretty that she—"

Flora smiled reluctantly. "If I were a man I could swear and *swear!*"

"Swear anyhow," suggested Billy encouragingly. "I'll show yuh how."

"And father away off in Klondyke," she said irrelevantly, passing over his generous offer, "and—and dead, for all we know! And she doesn't care—at *all!* She—"

Sympathy is good, but it has a disagreeable way of bringing all one's troubles to the front rather overwhelmingly. Flora suddenly dropped a plate back into the pan, leaned her face against the wall by the sink and began to cry in a tempestuous manner rather frightened Charming Billy Boyle, who had never before seen a grown woman cry real tears and sob like that.

He did what he could. He put his arms around her and held her close, and patted her hair and called her girlie, and laid his brown cheek against her wet one and told her to never mind and that it would be all right anyway, and that her father was probably picking away in his mine right then and wishing she was there to fry his bacon for him.

"I wish I was, too," she murmured, weaned from her weeping and talking into his coat. "If I'd known how—*she*—really was, I wouldn't ever have stayed. I'd have gone with father."

"And where would *I* come in?" he demanded selfishly, and so turned the conversation still farther from her trouble.

The water went stone cold in the dishpan and the fire died in the stove so that the frost spread a film over the thawed centre of the window panes. There is no telling when the dishes would have been washed that day if Mama Joy had not begun to pound energetically upon the floor—with the heel of a shoe, judging from the sound. Even that might not have proved a serious interruption; but Dill put his head in from the dining room and got as far as "That gray horse, William—" before he caught the significance of Flora perched on the knee of "William" and retreated hastily.

So Flora went to see what Mama Joy wanted, and Billy hurried somewhat guiltily out to find what was the matter with the gray horse, and practical affairs once more took control.

After that, Billy considered himself an engaged young man. He went back to his ditty and inquired frequently:

"Can she make a punkin pie, Billy boy, Billy Boy?"

and was very nearly the old, care-free Charming Billy of the line-camp. It is true that Mama Joy recovered disconcertingly that afternoon, and became once more ubiquitous, but Billy felt that nothing could cheat him of his joy, and remained cheerful under difficulties. He could exchange glances of much secret understanding with Flora, and he could snatch a hasty kiss, now and then, and when the chaperonage was too unremitting she could slip into his hands a hurriedly penciled note, filled with important nothings. Which made a bright spot in his life and kept Flora from thinking altogether of her father and fretting for some news of him.

Still, there were other things to worry him and to keep him from forgetting that the law of nature, which he had before defined to his own satisfaction, still governed the game. Storm followed storm with a monotonous regularity that was, to say the least, depressing, though to be sure there had been other winters like this, and not even Billy could claim that Nature was especially malignant.

But with Brown's new fence stretching for miles to the south and east of the open range near home, the drifting cattle brought up against it during the blinding blizzards and huddled there, freezing in the open, or else plodded stolidly along beside it until some washout or coulée too deep for crossing barred their way, so that the huddling and freezing was at best merely postponed. Billy, being quite alive to the exigencies of the matter, rode and rode, and with him rode Dill and the other two men when they had the leisure—which was not often, since the storms made much "shoveling" of hay necessary if they would keep the calves from dying by the dozen. They pushed the cattle away from the fences—to speak figuratively and colloquially—and drove them back to the open range until the next storm or cold north wind came and compelled them to repeat the process.

If Billy had had unlimited opportunity for lovemaking, he would not have had the time, for he spent hours in the saddle every day, unless the storm was too bitter for even him to face. There was the line-camp with which to keep in touch; he must ride often to the Bridger place—or he thought he must—to see how they were getting on. It worried him to see how large the "hospital bunch" was growing, and to see how many dark little mounds dotted the hollows, except when a new-fallen blanket of snow made them white—the carcasses of the calves that had "laid 'em down" already.

"Yuh ain't feeding heavy enough, boys," he told them once, before he quite realized how hard the weather was for stock.

"Yuh better ride around the hill and take a look at the stacks," suggested Jim Bleeker. "We're feeding heavy as we dare, Bill. If we don't get a let-up early we're going to be plumb out uh hay. There ain't been a week all together that the calves could feed away from the sheds. *That's* where the trouble lays."

Billy rode the long half-mile up the coulée to where the hay had mostly been stacked, and came back looking sober. "There's no use splitting the bunch and taking some to the Double-Crank," he said. "We need all the hay we've got over there. Shove 'em out on the hills and make 'em feed a little every day that's fit, and bank up them sheds and make 'em warmer. This winter's going to be one of our old steadies, the way she acts so far. It's sure a fright, the way this weather eats up the hay."

It was such incidents as these which weaned him again from his singing and his light-heartedness as the weeks passed coldly toward spring. He did not say very much about it to Dill, because he had a constitutional aversion to piling up agony ahead of him; besides, Dill could see for himself that the loss would be heavy, though just how heavy he hadn't the experience with which to estimate. As March came in with a blizzard and went, a succession of bleak days, into April, Billy knew more than he cared to admit even to himself. He would lie awake at night when the wind and snow raved over the land, and picture the bare open that he knew, with lean, Double-Crank stock drifting tail to the wind. He could fancy them coming up against this fence and that fence, which had not been there a year or two ago, and huddling there, freezing, cut off from the sheltered coulées that would have saved them.

"Damn these nesters and their fences!" He would grit his teeth at his helplessness, and then try to forget it all and think only of Flora.

CHAPTER XIX.
"I'm Not Your Wife Yet!"

Billy, coming back from the biggest town in the country, where he had gone to pick up another man or two for the round-up which was at hand, met the Pilgrim face to face as he was crossing the creek to go to the corrals. It was nearing sundown and it was Sunday, and those two details, when used in connection with the Pilgrim, seemed unpleasantly significant. Besides, Billy was freshly antagonistic because of something he had heard while he was away; instead of returning the Pilgrim's brazenly cheerful "Hello," he scowled and rode on without so much as giving a downward tilt to his chin. For Charming Billy Boyle was never inclined to diplomacy, or to hiding his feelings in any way unless driven to it by absolute necessity.

When he went into the house he saw that Flora had her hair done in a new way that was extremely pretty, and that she had on a soft, white silk shirt-waist with lots of lace zigzagged across—a waist hitherto kept sacred to dances and other glorious occasions—and a soft, pink bow pinned in her hair; all these things he mentally connected with the visit of the Pilgrim. When he turned to see a malicious light in the round, blue eyes of Mama Joy and a spiteful satisfaction in her very dimples, it suddenly occurred to him that he would certainly have something to say to Miss Flora. It was no comfort to know that all winter the Pilgrim had not been near, because all winter he had been away somewhere—rumor had it that he spent his winters in Iowa. Like the birds, he always returned with the spring.

Billy never suspected that Mama Joy read his face and left them purposely together after supper, though he was surprised when she arose from the table and said:

"Flora, you make Billy help you with the dishes. I've got a headache and I'm going to lie down."

At any rate, it gave him the opportunity he wanted.

"Are yuh going to let the Pilgrim hang around here this summer?" he demanded in his straight-from-the-shoulder fashion while he was drying the first cup.

"You mean Mr. Walland? I didn't know he ever 'hung around'." Flora was not meek, and Billy realized that, as he put it mentally, he had his work cut out for him to pull through without a quarrel.

"I mean the Pilgrim. And I call it hanging around when a fellow keeps running to see a girl that's got a loop on her already. I don't want to lay down the law to yuh, Girlie, but that blamed Siwash has got to keep away from here. He ain't fit for yuh to speak to—and I'd a told yuh before, only I didn't have any right—"

"Are you sure you have a right now?" The tone of Flora was sweet and calm and patient. "I'll tell you one thing, Charming Billy Boyle, Mr. Walland has never spoken one word against *you*. He—he *likes* you, and I don't think it's nice for you—"

"Likes me! Like hell he does!" snorted Billy, not bothering to choose nice words. "He'd plug me in the back like an Injun if he thought he could get off with it. I remember him when I hazed him away from line-camp, the morning after you stayed there, he promised faithful to kill me. Uh course, he won't, because he's afraid, but—I don't reckon yuh can call it liking—"

"*Why* did you 'haze him away,' as you call it, Billy? And kill his dog? It was a *nice* dog; I love dogs, and I don't see how any man—"

Billy flushed hotly. "I hazed him away because he insulted you," he said bluntly, not quite believing in her ignorance.

Flora, her hands buried deep in the soapsuds, looked at him round-eyed. "I never heard of that before," she said slowly. "When, Billy? And what did he—say?"

Billy stared at her. "*I* don't know what he said! I wouldn't think you'd need to ask. When I came in the cabin—I lied about getting lost from the trail—I turned around and came back, because I was afraid he might come before I could get back, and—when I came in, there was *something*. I could tell, all right. Yuh sat there behind the table looking like yuh was—well, kinda cornered. And he was—Flora, he *did* say something, or do something! He didn't act right to yuh. I could tell. *Didn't* he? Yuh needn't be afraid to tell me, Girlie. I give him a thrashing for it. What was it? I want to know." He did not realize how pugnacious was his pose, but he was leaning toward her with his face quite close, and his eyes were blue points of intensity. His hands, doubled and pressing hard on the table, showed white at the knuckles.

Flora rattled the dishes in the pan and laughed unsteadily. "Go to work, Billy Boy, and don't act stagey," she commanded lightly. "I'll tell you the exact truth—and that isn't anything to get excited over. Fred Walland came about three minutes before you did, and of course I didn't know he belonged there. I was afraid. He pushed open the door, and he was swearing a little at the ice there, where we threw out the dish water. I knew it wasn't you, and I got back in the corner. He came in and looked awfully stunned at seeing me and said, 'I beg your pardon, fair one'." She blushed and did not look up. "He said, 'I didn't know there was a lady present,' and put down the sack of stuff and looked at me for a minute or two without saying a word. He was just going to speak, I think, when you burst in. And that's all there was to it, Billy Boy. I was frightened because I didn't know who he was, and he *did* stare—but, so did you, Billy Boy, when I opened the door and walked in. You stared every bit as hard and long as Fred Walland did."

"But I'll bet I didn't have the same look in my face. Yuh wasn't scared of *me*," Billy asserted shrewdly.

"I was too! I was horribly scared—at first. So if you fought Fred Walland and killed his dog" (the reproach of her tone, then!) "because you imagined a lot that wasn't true, you ought to go straight and apologize."

"I don't *think* I will! Good Lord! Flora, do yuh think I don't *know* the stuff he's made of? He's a low-down, cowardly cur—the kind uh man that is always bragging about—" (Billy stuck there. With her big, innocent eyes looking up at him, he could not say "bragging about the women he's ruined," so he changed weakly) "about all he's done. He's a murderer that ought by rights t' be in the pen right now—"

"I think that will do, Billy!" she interrupted indignantly. "You know he couldn't help killing that man."

"I kinda believed that, too, till I run onto Jim Johnson up in Tower. You don't know Jim, but he's a straight man and wouldn't lie. Yuh remember, Flora, the Pilgrim told me the Swede pulled a knife on him. I stooped down and looked, and *I* didn't see no knife—nor gun, either. And I wasn't so blamed excited I'd be apt to pass up anything like that; I've seen men shot before, and pass out with their boots on, in more excitable ways than a little, plain, old killing. So I didn't see anything in the shape of a weapon. But when I come back, here lays a Colt forty-five right in plain sight, and the Pilgrim saying, 'He pulled a *gun* on me,' right on top uh telling me it was a *knife*. I thought at the time there was something queer about that, and about him not having a gun on him when I know he *always* packed one—like every other fool Pilgrim that comes West with the idea he's got to fight his way along from breakfast to supper, and sleep with his six-gun under his pillow!"

"And *I* know you don't like him, and you'd think he had some ulterior motive if he rolled his cigarette backward once! I don't see anything but just your dislike trying to twist things—"

"Well, hold on a minute! I got to talking with Jim, and we're pretty good friends. So he told me on the quiet that Gus Svenstrom gave him his gun to keep, that night. Gus was drinking, and said he didn't want to be packing it around for fear he might get foolish with it. Jim had it— Jim was tending bar that time in that little log saloon, in Hardup—when the Swede was killed. So it wasn't *the Swedes* gun on the ground—and if he borrowed one, which he wouldn't be apt to do, why didn't the fellow he got it from claim it?"

"And if all this is true, why didn't your friend come and testify at the hearing?" demanded Flora, her eyes glowing.

"It sounds to me exactly like a piece of spiteful old-woman gossip, and I don't believe a word of it!"

"Jim ain't a gossip. He kept his mouth shut because he didn't want to make trouble, and he was under the impression the Swede had borrowed a gun somewhere. Being half drunk, he could easy forget what he'd done with his own, and the Pilgrim put up such a straight story—"

"Fred told the truth. I know he did. I don't *believe* he had a gun that night, because—because I had asked him as a favor to please not carry one to dances and places. There, now! He'd do what I asked him to. I know he would. And I think you're just mean, to talk like this about him; and, mind you, if he wants to come here he can. I don't care if he comes *every day*!" She was so near to tears that her voice broke and kept her from saying more that was foolish.

"And I tell yuh, if he comes around here any more I'll chase him off the ranch with a club!" Billy's voice was not as loud as usual, but it was harsh and angry. "He ain't going to come here hanging around you—not while *I* can help it, and I guess I can, all right!" He threw down the dish towel, swept a cup off the table with his elbow when he turned, and otherwise betrayed human, unromantic rage. "Damn him, I wisht I'd chased him off long ago. Fred, eh? Hell! *I'll* Fred him! Yuh think I'm going to stand for him running after my girl? I'll kick him off the place. He ain't fit to speak to yuh, or look at yuh; his friendship's an insult to any decent woman. I'll mighty quick put a stop to—"

"Will Boyle, you don't *dare*! I'm not your wife yet, remember! I'm free to choose my own friends without asking leave of any one, and if I want Fred Walland to come here, he'll *come*, and it will take more than you to stop him. I—I'll write him a note, and ask him to dinner next Sunday. I—I'll *marry* him if I want to, Will Boyle, and you can't stop me! He—he wants me to, badly enough, and if you—"

Billy was gone, and the kitchen was rattling with the slam of the door behind him, before she had time to make any more declarations that would bring repentance afterward. She stood a minute, listening to see whether he would come back, and when he did not, she ran to the door, opened it hastily and looked. She saw Billy just in the act of swishing his quirt down on the flanks of Barney so that the horse almost cleared the creek in one bound. Flora caught her breath and gave a queer little sob. She watched him, wide-eyed and white, till he was quite out of sight and then went in and shut the door upon the quiet, early spring twilight.

As for Billy, he was gone to find the Pilgrim. Just what he would do when he did find him was not quite plain, because he was promising himself so many deeds of violence that no man could possibly perform them all upon one victim. At the creek, he was going to "shoot him like a coyote." A quarter of a mile farther, he would "beat his damn' head off," and, as if those were not deaths sufficient, he was after that determined to "take him by the heels and snap his measly head off like yuh would a grass snake!"

Threatened as he was, the Pilgrim nevertheless escaped, because Billy did not happen to come across him before his rage had cooled to reason. He rode on to Hardup, spent the night there swallowing more whisky than he had drunk before in six months, and after that playing poker with a recklessness that found a bitter satisfaction in losing and thus proving how vilely the world was using him, and went home rather unsteadily at sunrise and slept heavily in the bunk-house all that day. For Billy Boyle was distressingly human in his rages as in his happier moods, and was not given to gentle, picturesque melancholy and to wailing at the silent stars.

CHAPTER XX.
The Shadow Lies Long.

What time he was compelled to be in the house, in the few remaining days before round-up, he avoided Flora or was punctiliously polite. Only once did he address her directly by name, and then he called her Miss Bridger with a stiff formality that made Mama Joy dimple with spiteful satisfaction. Flora replied by calling him Mr. Boyle, and would not look at him.

Then it was all in the past, and Billy was out on the range learning afresh how sickeningly awry one's plans may go. As mile after mile of smiling grass-land was covered by the sweep of the Double-Crank circles, the disaster pressed more painfully upon him. When the wagons had left the range the fall before, Billy had estimated roughly that eight or nine thousand head of Double-Crank stock wandered at will in the open. But with the gathering and the calf-branding he knew that the number had shrunk woefully. Of the calves he had left with their mothers in the fall, scarce one remained; of the cows themselves he could find not half, and the calf-branding was becoming a grim joke among the men.

"Eat hearty," they would sometimes banter one another. "We got to buckle down and *work* this afternoon. They's three calves milling around out there waiting to be branded!"

"Aw, come off! There ain't but two," another would bellow.

If it were not quite as bad as that, it was in all conscience bad enough, and when they swung up to the reservation line and found there a fence in the making, and saw the Indian cowboys at work throwing out all but reservation stock, Billy mentally threw up his hands and left the outfit in Jim Bleeker's charge while he rode home to consult Dill. For Billy Boyle, knowing well his range-lore, could see nothing before the Double-Crank but black failure.

"It begins to look, Dilly," he began, "as though I've stuck yuh on this game. Yuh staked the wrong player; yuh should uh backed the man that stacked the deck on me. There's hell to pay on the range, Dilly. Last winter sure put a crimp in the range-stuff—*that's* what I come to tell yuh. I knew it would cut into the bunch. I could tell by the way things was going close around here—but I didn't look for it to be as bad as it is. And they're fencing in the reservation this spring—that cuts off a big chunk uh mighty good grazing and winter shelter along all them creeks. And I see there's quite a bunch uh grangers come in, since I was along east uh here. They've got cattle turned on the range, and there's half a dozen shacks scattered—"

"Mr. Brown is selling off tracts of land with water-rights—under that big ditch, you understand. He's working a sort of colonization scheme, as near as I can find out. He is also fencing more land to the north and west—toward Hardup, in fact. I believe they already have most of the posts set. We'll soon be surrounded, William. And while we're upon the subject of our calamities, I might state that we shall not be able to do any irrigating this season. Mr. Brown is running his ditch half full and has been for some little time. He kindly leaves enough for our stock to drink, however!"

"Charitable old cuss—that same Brown! I was figuring on the hay to kinda ease through next winter. Do yuh know, Dilly, the range is just going t' be a death-trap, with all them damn fences for the stock to drift into. Another winter half as bad as the last one was will sure put the finishing touches to the Double-Crank—unless we get busy and *do* something." Billy, his face worn and his eyes holding that tired look which comes of nights sleepless and of looking long upon trouble, turned and began to pull absently at a splintered place in the gatepost. He had stopped Dill at the corral to have a talk with him, because to him the house was as desolate as if a dear one lay dead inside. Flora was at home—trust his eyes to see her face appear briefly at the window when he rode up!—but he could not yet quite endure to face her and her cold greeting.

Dill, looking to Billy longer and lanker and mere melancholy than ever, caressed his chin meditatively and regarded Billy in his wistful, half-deprecating way. With the bitter knowledge that his castle, and with it Dill's fortune, was toppling, Billy could hardly bear to meet that look. And he had planned such great things, and had meant to make Dilly a millionaire!

"What would you advise, William, under the present unfavorable conditions?" asked Dill hesitatingly.

"Oh, I dunno. I've laid awake nights tryin' to pick a winning card. If it was me, and me alone, I'd pull stakes and hunt another range—and I'd go gunning after the first damn' man that stuck up a post to hang barb-wire on. But after me making such a rotten-poor job uh running the Double-Crank, I don't feel called on to lay down the law to anybody!"

"If you will permit me to pass judgment, William, I will say that you have shown an ability for managing men and affairs which I consider remarkable; *quite* remarkable. You, perhaps, do not go deep enough in searching for the cause of our misfortunes. It is not bad management or the hard winter, or Mr. Brown, even—and I blame myself bitterly for failing to read aright the 'handwriting on the wall,' to quote scripture, which I seldom do. If you have ever read history, William, you must know—even if you have *not* read history you should know from observation—how irresistible is the march of progress; how utterly futile it is for individuals to attempt to defy it. I should have known that the shadow of a great change has fallen on the West—the West of the wide, open ranges and the cattle and the cowboy who tends them. I should have seen it, but I did not. I was culpably careless.

"Brown saw it, and that, William, is why he sold the Double-Crank to me. *He* saw that the range was doomed, and instead of being swallowed with the open range he very wisely changed his business; he became allied with Progress, and he was in the front rank. While we are being 'broken' on the wheel of evolutionary change, he will make his millions—"

"Damn him!" gritted Billy savagely, under his breath.

"He is to be admired, William. Such a man is bound in the very nature of things to succeed. It is the range and—and you, William, and those like you, that must go. It is hard—no doubt it is *extremely* hard, but it is as irresistible as—as death itself. Civilization is compelled to crush the old order of things that it may fertilize the soil out of which grows the new. It is so in plant life, and in the life of humans, also.

"I am explaining at length, William, so that you will quite understand why I do not think it wise to follow your suggestion. As I say, it is not Brown, or the fences, or anything of that sort—taken in a large sense—which is forcing us to the wall. It is the press of natural progress, the pushing farther and farther of civilization. We might move to a more unsettled portion of the country and delay for a time the ultimate crushing. We could not avoid it entirely; we might, at best, merely postpone it.

"My idea is to gather everything and sell for as high a price as possible. Then—perhaps it would be well to follow Mr. Brown's example, and turn this place into a farm; or sell it, also, and try something else. What do you think, William?"

But Billy, his very soul sickening under the crushing truth of what Dill in his prim grammatical way was saying, did not answer at all. He was picking blindly, mechanically at the splinter, his face shaded by his worn, gray hat; and he was thinking irrelevantly how a condemned man must feel when they come to him in his cell and in formal words read aloud his death-warrant. One sentence was beating monotonously in his brain: "It is the range—and you, William, and those like you—that must go." It was not a mere loss of dollars or of cattle or even of hopes; it was the rending, the tearing from him of a life he loved; it was the taking of the range—land—the wide, beautiful, weather-worn land—big and grand in its freedom of all that was narrow and sordid, and it was cutting and scarring it, harnessing it to the petty uses of a class he despised with all the frank egotism of a man who loves his own outlook; giving it over to the "nester" and the "rube" and burying the sweet-smelling grasses with plows. It was—he could not, even in the eloquence of his utter despair, find words for all it meant to him.

"I should, of course, leave the details to you, so far as getting the most out of the stock is concerned. I have been thinking of this for some little time, and your report of range conditions merely confirms my own judgment. If you think we would better sell at once—"

"I'd let 'em go till fall," said Billy lifelessly, snapping the splinter back into place and reaching absently for his tobacco and papers. "They're bound to pick up a lot—and what's left is mostly big, husky steers that'll make prime beef. With decent prices yuh ought to pull clear uh what yuh owe Brown, and have a little left. I didn't make anything like a count; they was so thin I handled 'em as light as I could and get the calves branded—what few there was. But I feel tolerable safe in saying you can round up six—well, between six and seven thousand head. At a fair price yuh ought to pull clear."

"Well, after dinner—"

"I can't stay for dinner, Dilly. I—there's—I've got to ride over here a piece—I'll catch up a fresh hoss and start right off. I—" He went rather hurriedly after his rope, as hurriedly caught the horse that was handiest and rode away at a lope. But he did not go so very far. He just galloped over the open range to a place where, look where he might, he could not see a fence or sign of habitation (and it wrung the heart of him that he must ride into a coulée to find such a place), got down from his horse and lay a long, long while in the grass with his hat pulled over his face.

For the first time in years the Fourth of July saw Billy in camp and in his old clothes. He had not hurried the round-up—on the contrary he had been guilty of dragging it out unnecessarily by all sorts of delays and leisurely methods—simply because he hated to return to the ranch and be near Flora. The Pilgrim he meant to settle with, but he felt that he could wait; he hadn't much enthusiasm even for a fight, these days.

But, after all, he could not consistently keep the wagons forever on the range, so he camped them just outside the pasture fence; which was far enough from the house to give him some chance of not being tormented every day by the sight of her, and yet was close enough for all practical purposes. And here it was that Dill came with fresh news.

"Beef is falling again, William," he announced when he had Billy quite to himself. "Judging from present indications, it will go quite as low as last fall—even lower, perhaps. If it does, I fail to see how we can ship with any but disastrous financial results."

"Well, what yuh going to do, then?" Billy spoke more irritably than would have been possible a year ago. "Yuh can't winter again and come out with anything but another big loss. Yuh haven't even got hay to feed what few calves there is. And, as I told yuh, the way the fences are strung from hell to breakfast, the stock's bound to die off like poisoned flies every storm that comes."

"I have kept that in mind, William. I saw that I should be quite unable to make a payment this fall, so I went to Mr. Brown to make what arrangements I could. To be brief, William, Brown has offered to buy back this place and the stock, on much the same terms he offered me. I believe he wants to put this section of land under irrigation from his ditch and exploit it with the rest; the cattle he can turn into his immense fields until they can be shipped at a profit. However, that is not our affair and need not concern us.

"He will take the stock as they run, at twenty-one dollars a head. If, as you estimate, there are somewhere in the neighborhood of six thousand, that will dear me of all indebtedness and leave a few thousands with which to start again—at something more abreast of the times, I hope. I am rather inclined to take the offer. What do you think of it, William?"

"I guess yuh can't do any better. Twenty-one dollars a head as they run—and everything else thrown in, uh course?"

"That is the way I bought it, yes," said Dill.

"Well, we ought to scare up six thousand, if we count close. I know old Brown fine; he'll hold yuh right down t' what yuh turn over, and he'll tally so close he'll want to dock yuh if a critter's shy one horn—damn him. That's why I was wishing you'd bought that way, instead uh lumping the price and taking chances. Only, uh course, I knew just about what was on the range."

"Then I will accept the offer. I have been merely considering it until I saw you. And perhaps it will be as well to go about it immediately."

"It's plenty early," objected Billy. "I was going to break some more hosses for the saddle-bunch—but I reckon I'll leave 'em now for Brown to bust. And for *God*-sake, Dilly, once yuh get wound up here, go on back where yuh come from. If the range is going—and they's no use saying it ain't—this ain't going to be no place for any white man." Which was merely Billy's prejudice speaking.

CHAPTER XXI.
The End of the Double-Crank.

Dill himself rode on that last round-up. Considering that it was all new to him, he made a remarkably good record for himself among the men, who were more than once heard to remark that "Dill-pickle's sure making a hand!" Wherever Billy went—and in those weeks Billy rode and worked with a feverish intensity that was merely a fight against bitter thinking—Dill's stirrup clacked close alongside. He was silent, for the most part, but sometimes he talked reminiscently of Michigan and his earlier life there. Seldom did he refer to the unhappy end of the Double-Crank, or to the reason why they were riding from dawn to dusk, sweeping together all the cattle within the wide circle of riders and later cutting out every Double-Crank animal and holding them under careful herd.

Even when they went with the first twelve hundred and turned them over to Brown and watched his careful counting, Dill made no comment upon the reason for it beyond one sentence. He read the receipt over slowly before laying it methodically in the proper compartment of his long red-leather book, and drew his features into his puckered imitation of a smile. "Mr. Brown has counted just twenty-one dollars more into my pocket than I expected," he remarked. "He tallied one more than you did, William. I ought to hold that out of your wages, young man."

Rare as were Dill's efforts at joking, even this failed to bring more than a slight smile to the face of Charming

Billy Boyle. He was trying to look upon it all as a mere incident, a business matter, pure and simple, but he could not. While he rode the wide open reaches, there rode with him the keen realization that it was the end. For him the old life on the range was dead—for had not Dill made him see it so? And did not every raw-red fencepost proclaim anew its death? For every hill and every coulée he buried something of his past and wept secretly beside the grave. For every whiff of breakfast that mingled with the smell of clean air in the morning came a pang of homesickness for what would soon be only a memory.

He was at heart a dreamer—was Charming Billy Boyle; perhaps an idealist—possibly a sentimentalist. He had never tried to find a name for the side of his life that struck deepest. He knew that the ripple of a meadow-lark swinging on a weed against the sunrise, with diamond-sparkles all on the grass around, gripped him and hurt him vaguely with its very sweetness. He knew that he loved to sit alone and look away to a far skyline and day-dream. He had always known that, for it had been as much a part of his life as sleeping.

So now it was as if a real, tangible shadow lay on the range. He could see it always lengthening before him, and always he must ride within its shade. After a while it would grow quite black, and the range and the cattle and the riding over hills and into coulées untamed would all be blotted out; dead and buried deep in the past, and with the careless, plodding feet of the plowman trampling unthinkingly upon the grave. It was a tragedy to Charming

Billy Boyle; it was as if the range-land were a woman he loved well, and as if civilization were the despoiler, against whom he had no means of defense.

All this—and besides, Flora. He had not spoken to her for two months. He had not seen her even, save for a passing glimpse now and then at a distance. He had not named her to any man, or asked how she did—and yet there had not been an hour when he had not longed for her. She had told him she would marry the Pilgrim (she had *not* said that, but Billy in his rage had so understood her) and that he could not stop her. He wouldn't *try* to stop her. But he would one day settle with the Pilgrim—settle to the full. And he wanted her—*wanted* her!

They had taken the third herd in to Brown, and were back on the range; Billy meaning to make a last sweep around the outer edges and gather in what was left—the stragglers that had been missed before. There would not be many, he knew from experience; probably not more than a hundred or two all told, even with Billy anxious to make the count as large as possible.

He was thinking about it uneasily and staring out across the wide coulée to the red tumble of clouds, that had strange purples and grays and dainty violet shades here and there. Down at the creek Dill was trying to get a trout or two more before it grew too dark for them to rise to the raw beef he was swishing through the riffle, and an impulse to have the worst over at once and be done drove Billy down to interrupt.

"Yuh won't get any more there," he said, by way of making speech.

"I just then had a bite, William," reproved Dill, and swung the bait in a wide circle for another awkward cast. He was a persistent soul, was Dill, when once he got started in a given direction.

Billy, dodging the red morsel of meat, sat down on a grassy hummock. "Aw, come and set down, Dilly," he urged wearily. "I want to tell yuh something."

"If it's about the cook being out of evaporated cream, William, I have already been informed twice. Ah-h! I almost had one then!"

"Aw, thunder! yuh think I'm worrying over canned cream? What I want to say may not be more important, but when yuh get fishing enough I'll say it anyhow." He watched Dill moodily, and then lifted his eyes to stare at the gorgeous sky—as though there would be no more sunsets when the range-life was gone, and he must needs fill well his memory for the barren years ahead.

When Dill flopped a six-inch trout against his ear, so steeped was he in bitterness that he merely said, "Aw, hell!" wearily and hunched farther along on the hummock.

"I really beg your pardon, William. From the vicious strike he made, I was convinced that he weighed at least half a pound, and exerted more muscular force than was quite necessary. When one hasn't a reel it is impossible to play them properly, and it is the first quick pull that one must depend upon. I'm very sorry—"

"Sure. Don't mention it, Dilly. Say, how many cattle have yuh got receipts for, to date—if it ain't too much trouble?"

"No trouble at all, William. I have an excellent memory for figures. Four thousand, three hundred and fifteen. Ah-h! See how instinct inspires him to flop always toward the water! Did you ever—"

"Well, yes, I've saw a fish flop toward the water once or twicet before now. It sure is a great sight, Dilly!" He did not understand Dill these days, and wondered a good deal at his manifest indifference to business cares. It never occurred to him that Dill, knowing quite well how hard the trouble pressed upon his foreman, was only trying in his awkward way to lighten it by not seeming to think it worth worrying over.

"I hate to mention trifles at such a time, Dilly, but I thought maybe yuh ought to know that we won't be able to scare up more than a couple uh hundred more cattle, best we can do. We're bound to fall a lot short uh what I estimated—and I ain't saying nothing about the fine job uh guessing I done! If we bring the total up to forty-five hundred, we'll do well."

Dill took plenty of time to wind the line around his willow pole. "To use your own expressive phraseology, William," he said, when he had quite finished and had laid the pole down on the bank, "that will leave me in one hell-of-a-hole!"

"That's what I thought," Billy returned apathetically.

"Well, I must take these up to the cook." Dill held up the four fish he had caught. "I'll think the matter over,

William, and I thank you for telling me. Of course you will go on and gather what there are."

"Sure," agreed Billy tonelessly, and followed Dill back to camp and went to bed.

At daybreak it was raining, and Billy after the manner of cowboys slept late; for there would be no riding until the weather cleared, and there being no herd to hold, there would be none working save the horse-wrangler, the night-hawk and cook. It was the cook who handed him a folded paper and a sealed envelope when he did finally appear for a cup of coffee. "Dill-pickle left 'em for yuh," he said.

Billy read the note—just a few lines, with a frown of puzzlement.

Dear William: Business compels my absence for a time. I hope you will go on with your plans exactly as if I were with you. I am leaving a power-of-attorney which will enable you to turn over the stock and transact any other business that may demand immediate attention, in case I am detained.

Yours truly,

Alexander P. Dill

It was queer, but Billy did not waste much time in wondering. He rounded up the last of the Double-Cranks, drove them to Brown's place and turned them over, with the home ranch, the horses, and camp outfit—"made a clean sweep uh the whole damn', hoodooed works," was the way he afterward put it. He had expected that Dill would be there to attend to the last legal forms, but there was no sign of him or from him. He had been seen to take the eastbound train at Tower, and the rest was left to guessing.

"He must uh known them two-hundred odd wouldn't square the deal," argued Billy loyally to himself. "So uh course he'll come back and fix it up. But what I'm to do about payin' off the boys gets me." For two hours he worried, mentally in the dark. Then he hit upon an expedient that pleased him. He told Brown he would need to keep a few of the saddle-horses for a few days, and he sent the boys—those of them who did not transfer their valuable services to Brown upon the asking—over to the Bridger place to wait there until further orders.

Also, he rode reluctantly to the Double-Crank ranch, wondering, as he had often done in the past few weeks, what would become of Flora and Mama Joy. So far as he knew, they had not heard a word as to whether Bridger was alive or dead, and if they had friends or family to whom they might turn, he had never heard either mention them. If Dill had been there he would have left it to him; but Dill was gone, and there was no knowing when he would be back, and it devolved upon Billy to make some arrangements for the women, or at the least offer his services—and it was, under the circumstances, quite the most unpleasant duty thus far laid upon him.

He knew they had been left there at the ranch when round-up started, because Dill had said something about leaving a gentle horse or two for them to ride. Whether they were still there he did not know, although he could easily have asked Spikes, who had been given charge of the ranch while Dill was away on the range. He supposed the Pilgrim would be hanging around, as usual—not that it made much difference, though, except that he hated the thought of a disagreeable scene before the women.

He rode slowly up to the corral gate, turned his horse inside and fastened the chain just as he had done a thousand times before—only this would be the last time. His tired eyes went from one familiar object to another, listlessly aware of the regret he should feel but too utterly wearied of sorrow to feel much of anything. No one seemed to be about, and the whole place had an atmosphere of desolation that almost stirred him to a heartache—almost.

He went on to the house. There were some signs of life there, and some sound. In the very doorway he met old Bridger himself, but he could not even feel much surprise at seeing him there. He said hello, and when he saw the other's hand stretching out to meet him, he clasped it indifferently. Behind her husband, Mama Joy flashed at him a look he did not try to interpret—of a truth it was rather complex, with a little of several emotions—and he lifted his hat a half-inch from his forehead in deference to her sex. Flora, he thanked God dully, he did not see at all.

He stayed perhaps ten minutes listening impersonally to Bridger, who talked loudly and enthusiastically of his plans. At the time they did not seem to concern him at all, though they involved taking Flora and Mama Joy away to Seattle to spend the winter, and in the spring moving them on to some place in the North—a place that sounded strange in the ears of Billy, and was straightway forgotten. After that he went to his room and packed what few things he wanted; and they were not many, because in his present mood nothing mattered and nothing seemed to him of much value—not even life. He was more careful of Dill's belongings, and packed everything he could find that was his. They were not scattered, for Dill was a methodical man and kept things in their places instinctively.

He paused over but one object—"The Essays of Elia," which had somehow fallen behind a trunk. Standing there in the middle of Dill's room, he turned the little blue book absently in his hand. There was dust upon the other side, and he wiped it off, manlike, with a sweep of his forearm. He looked at the trunk; he had just locked it with much straining of muscles and he hated to open it again. He looked at the book again. He seemed to see Dill slumped loosely down in the old rocker, a slippered foot dangling before him, reading solemnly from this same little blue book, the day he came to tell him about the ditch, and that he must lease all the land he could—the day when the shadow of passing first touched the range-land. At least, the day when he had first seen it there. He turned a few leaves thoughtfully, heard Flora's voice asking a question in the kitchen, and thrust the book hastily into his pocket. "Dilly'll want it, I expect," he muttered. He glanced quickly, comprehensively around him to make sure that he had missed nothing, turned toward the open front door and went out hurriedly, because he thought he heard a woman's step in the dining room and he did not want to see anybody, not even Flora—least of all, Flora!

"I'll send a rig out from town for the stuff that's ours," he called back to Bridger, who came to the kitchen door and called after him that he better wait and have some supper. "You'll be here till to-morrow or next day; it ain't likely I'll be back; yuh say Dill settled up with the—women, so—there's nothing left to do."

If he had known—but how could he know that Flora was watching him wistfully from the front porch, when he never once looked toward the house after he reached the stable?

CHAPTER XXII.
Settled In Full.

On a lonely part of the trail to town—queerly, it was when he was rounding the low, barren hill where he and Dill had first met—he took out his brand-book and went over the situation. It was Barney he rode, and Barney could be trusted to pace along decorously with the reins twisted twice around the saddle-horn, so Billy gave no thought to his horse but put his whole mind on the figures. He was not much used to these things; beyond keeping tally of the stock at branding and shipping time and putting down what details of his business he dared not trust to memory, a pencil was strange to his fingers. But the legal phrases in the paper left by Dill and signed by the cook and night-hawk as witnesses gave him a heavy sense of responsibility that everything should be settled exactly right. So now he went over the figures slowly, adding them from the top down and from the bottom up, to make sure he had the totals correct. He wished they were wrong; they might then be not quite so depressing.

"Lemme see, now. I turned over 4,523 head uh stock, all told (hell of a fine job uh guessing I done! Me saying there'd be over six thousand!) That made $94,983. And accordin' to old Brown—and I guess he had it framed up correct—Dilly owes him $2,217 yet, instead uh coming out with enough to start some other business. It's sure queer, the way figures always come out little when yuh want 'em big, and big when yuh want 'em little! Them debts now—

they could stand a lot uh shavin' down. Twelve thousand dollars and interest, to the bank—I can't do a darn thing about them twelve thousand. If Dilly hadn't gone and made a cast-iron agreement I coulda held old Brown up for a few thousand more, on account uh the increase in saddle-stock. I'd worked that bunch up till it sure was a dandy lot uh hosses—but what yuh going to do?"

He stared dispiritedly out across the brown prairie. "I'd oughta put Dilly next to that, only I never thought about it at the time, and I was so dead sure the range-stuff—And there's the men, got to have their money right away quick, so's they can hurry up and blow it in! If Dilly ain't back to-night, or I don't hear from him, I reckon I'll have to draw m' little old wad out uh the bank and pay the sons-uh-guns. I sure ain't going to need it to buy dishes and rocking chairs and pictures—and I was going t' git her a piano—oh, hell!"

He still rode slowly, after that, but he did not bother over the figures that stood for Dilly's debts. He sat humped over the saddle-horn like an old man and stared at the trail and at the forefeet of Barney coming down *pluck, pluck* with leisurely regularity in the dust. Just so was Charming Billy Boyle trampling down the dreams that had been so sweet in the dreaming, and leveling ruthlessly the very foundations of the fair castle he had builded in the air for Dill and himself—and one other, with the fairest, highest, most secret chambers for that Other. And as he rode, the face of him was worn and the blue eyes of him sombre and dull; and his mouth, that had lost utterly the humorous, care-free quirk at the corners, was bitter, and straight, and hard.

He had started out with such naïve assurance to succeed, and—he had failed so utterly, so hopelessly, with not even a spectacular crash to make the failing picturesque. He had done the best that was in him, and even now that it was over he could not quite understand how everything, *everything* could go like that; how the Double-Crank and Flora—how the range, even, had slipped from him. And now Dill was gone, too, and he did not even know where, or if he would ever come back.

He would pay the men; he had, with a surprising thrift, saved nearly a thousand dollars in the bank at Tower. That, to be sure, was when he had Flora to save for; since then he had not had time or opportunity to spend it foolishly. It would take nearly every dollar; the way he had figured it, he would have just twenty-three dollars left for himself—and he would have the little bunch of horses he had in his prosperity acquired for the pure love of owning a good horse. He would sell the horses, except Barney and one to pack his bed, and he would drift—drift just as do the range-cattle when a blizzard strikes them in the open. Billy felt like a stray. His range was gone—gone utterly. He would roll his bed and drift; and perhaps, somewhere, he could find a stretch of earth as God had left it, unscarred by fence and plow, undefiled by cabbages and sugar-beets (Brown's new settlers were going strong on sugar-beets).

"Well, it's all over but the shouting," he summed up grimly when Hardup came in sight. "I'll pay off the men and turn 'em loose—all but Jim. Somebody's got to stay with the Bridger place till Dilly shows up, seeing that's all he's got left after the clean-up. The rest uh the debts can wait. Brown's mortgage ain't due yet" (Billy had his own way of looking at financial matters) "and the old Siwash ain't got any kick comin' if he never gets another cent out uh Dilly. The bank ain't got the cards to call Dilly now, for his note ain't due till near Christmas. So I reckon all I got to do after I pay the boys is take m' little old twenty-three plunks, and my hosses—if I can't sell 'em right off—and pull out for God-knows-where-and-I-don't-care-a-damn!"

Charming Billy Boyle had done all that he had planned to do, except that he had not yet pulled out for the place he had named picturesquely for himself. Much as at the beginning, he was leaning heavily upon the bar in the Hardup Saloon, and his hat was pushed back on his head; but he was not hilarious to the point of singing about "the young thing," and he was not, to any appreciable extent, enjoying himself. He was merely adding what he considered the proper finishing touch to his calamities. He was spinning silver dollars, one by one, across the bar to the man with the near-white apron, and he was endeavoring to get the worth of them down his throat. To be sure, he was being assisted, now and then, by several acquaintances; but considering the fact that a man's stomach has certain well-defined limitations, he was doing very well, indeed.

When he had spun the twenty-third dollar to the bartender, Billy meant to quit drinking for the present; after that, he was not quite clear as to his intentions, farther than "forking his hoss and pulling out" when there was no more to be done. He felt uneasily that between his present occupation and the pulling-out process lay a duty unperformed, but until the door swung open just as he was crying, "Come on, fellows," he had not been able to name it.

The Pilgrim it was who entered jauntily; the Pilgrim, who had not chanced to meet Billy once during the summer, and so was not aware that the truce between them was ended for good and all. He knew that Billy had not at any time been what one might call cordial, but that last stare of displeasure when they met in the creek at the Double-Crank, he had set down to a peevish mood. Under the circumstances, it was natural that he should walk up to the bar with the rest. Under the circumstances, it was also natural that Billy should object to this unexpected and unwelcome guest, and that the vague, unperformed duty should suddenly flash into his mind clear, and well-defined, and urgent.

"Back up, Pilgrim," was his quiet way of making known his purpose. "Yuh can't drink on *my* money, old-timer, nor use a room that I'm honoring with my presence. Just right now, I'm *here*. It's up to you to back out—*away* out—clean outside and across the street."

The Pilgrim did not move.

Billy had been drinking, but his brain was not of the stuff that fuddles easily, and he was not, as the Pilgrim believed, drunk. His eyes when he stared hard at the Pilgrim were sober eyes, sane eyes—and something besides.

"I said it," he reminded softly, when men had quit shuffling their feet and the room was very still.

"I don't reckon yuh know what yuh said," the Pilgrim retorted, laughing uneasily and shifting his gaze a bit. "What they been doping yuh with, Bill? There ain't any quarrel between you and me no more." His tone was abominably, condescendingly tolerant, and his look was the look which a mastiff turns wearily upon a hysterical toy-terrier yapping foolishly at his knees. For the Pilgrim had changed much in the past year and more during which men had respected him because he was not considered quite safe to trifle with. According to the reputation they gave him, he had killed a man who had tried to kill him, and he could therefore afford to be pacific upon occasion.

Billy stared at him while he drew a long breath; a breath which seemed to press back a tangible weight of hatred and utter contempt for the Pilgrim; a breath while it seemed that he must kill him there and stamp out the very semblance of humanity from his mocking face.

"Yuh don't know of any quarrel between you and me? Yuh say yuh don't?" Billy's voice trembled a little, because of the murder-lust that gripped him. "Well, pretty soon, I'll start in and tell yuh all about it—maybe. Right now, I'm going t' give a new one—one that yuh can easy name and do what yuh damn' please about." Whereupon he did as he had done once before when the offender had been a sheepherder. He stepped quickly to one side of the Pilgrim, emptied a glass down inside his collar, struck him sharply across his grinning mouth, and stepped back—back until there were eight or ten feet between them.

"That's the only way *my* whisky can go down *your* neck!" he said.

Men gasped and moved hastily out of range, never doubting what would happen next. Billy himself knew—or thought he knew—and his hand was on his gun, ready to pull it and shoot; hungry—waiting for an excuse to fire.

The Pilgrim had given a bellow that was no word at all, and whirled to come at Billy; met his eyes, wavered and hesitated, his gun in his hand and half-raised to fire.

Billy, bent on giving the Pilgrim a fair chance, waited another second; waited and saw fear creep into the bold eyes of the Pilgrim; waited and saw the inward cringing of the man. It was like striking a dog and waiting for the spring at your throat promised by his snarling defiance, and then seeing the fire go from his eyes as he grovels, cringingly confessing you his master, himself a cur.

What had been hate in the eyes of Billy changed slowly to incredulous contempt. "Ain't that enough?" he cried disgustedly. "My God, ain't yuh *man* enough—Have I got to take yuh by the ear and slit your gullet like they stick pigs—or else let yuh *go*? What *are* yuh, anyhow? Shall I give my gun to the bar-keep and go out where it's dark?

Will yuh be scared to tackle me then?" He laughed and watched the yellow terror creep over the face of the Pilgrim at the taunt. "What's wrong with your gun? Ain't it working good to-night? Ain't it loaded?

"Heavens and earth! What else have I got to do before you'll come alive? You've been living on your rep as a bad man to monkey with, and pushing out your wishbone over it for quite a spell, now—why don't yuh get busy and collect another bunch uh admiration from these fellows? *I* ain't no lightning-shot man! Papa Death don't roost on the end uh my six-gun—or I never suspicioned before that he did; but from the save-me-quick look on yuh, I believe yuh'd faint plumb away if I let yuh take a look at the end uh my gun, with the butt-end toward yuh!

"Honest t' God, Pilgrim, I won't try to get in ahead uh yuh! I couldn't if I tried, because mine's at m' belt yet and I ain't so swift. Come on! Please—*purty* please!" Billy looked around the room and laughed. He pointed his finger mockingly "Ain't he a peach of a Bad Man, boys? Ain't yuh proud uh his acquaintance? I reckon I'll have to turn my back before he'll cut loose. Yuh know, he's just aching t' kill me—only he don't want me to know it when he does! He's afraid he might hurt m' feelings!"

He swung back to the Pilgrim, went close, and looked at him impertinently, his head on one side. He reached out deliberately with his hand, and the Pilgrim ducked and cringed away. "Aw, look here!" he whined. "*I* ain't done nothing to yuh, Bill!"

Billy's hand dropped slowly and hung at his side. "Yuh—damned—coward!" he gritted. "Yuh know yuh wouldn't get any more than an even break with me, and that ain't enough for yuh. You're afraid to take a chance. You're afraid—God!" he cried suddenly, swept out of his mockery by the rage within. "And I can't kill yuh! Yuh won't show nerve enough to give me a chance! Yuh won't even *fight*, will yuh?"

He leaned and struck the Pilgrim savagely. "Get out uh my sight, then! Get out uh town! Get clean out uh the country! Get out among the coyotes—they're nearer your breed than men!" For every sentence there was a stinging blow—a blow with the flat of his hand, driving the Pilgrim back, step by step, to the door. The Pilgrim, shielding his head with an uplifted arm, turned then and bolted out into the night.

Behind him were men who stood ashamed for their manhood, not caring to look straight at one another with so sickening an example before them of the craven coward a man may be. In the doorway, Billy stood framed against the yellow lamplight, a hand pressing hard against the casings while he leaned and hurled curses in a voice half-sobbing with rage.

It was so that Dill found him when he came looking. When he reached out and laid a big-knuckled hand gently on his arm, Billy shivered and stared at him in a queer, dazed fashion for a minute.

"Why—hello, Dilly!" he said then, and his voice was hoarse and broken. "Where the dickens did *you* come from?" Without a word Dill, still holding him by the arm, led him unresisting away.

CHAPTER XXIII.
Oh, Where Have You Been, Charming Billy?

Presently they were in the little room which Dill had kept for himself by the simple method of buying the shack that held it, and Billy was drinking something which Dill poured out for him and which steadied him wonderfully.

"If you are not feeling quite yourself, William, perhaps we would do better to postpone our conversation until morning," Dill was saying while he rocked awkwardly, his hands folded loosely together, his elbows on the rocker—arms and his round, melancholy eyes regarding Billy solemnly. "I wanted to ask how you came out—with the Double-Crank."

"Go ahead; I'm all right," said Billy. "I aim to hit the trail by sun-up, so we'll have our little say now." He made him a cigarette and looked wistfully at Dill, while he felt for a match. "Go ahead. What do yuh want to know the worst?"

"Well, I did not see Brown, and it occurred to me that after I left you must have gathered more stock than you anticipated. I discovered from the men that you have paid them off. I rode out there to-day, you know. I arrived about two hours after you had left."

"You're still in the hole on the cow-business," Billy stated flatly, as if there were no use in trying to soften the telling. "Yuh owe Brown two thousand odd dollars. I turned in a few over two hundred head—I've got it all down here, and yuh can see the exact figure yourself. Yuh didn't show up, and I didn't want to hold the men and let their time run on and nothing doing to make it pay, so I give 'em their money and let 'em off—all but Jim Bleeker. I didn't pay him, because I wanted him to look after things at the Bridger place till yuh got back, and I knew if I give him any money he'd burn the earth getting to where he could spend it. He's a fine fellow when he's broke—Jim is."

"But I owed the men for several months' work. Where did you raise the amount, William?" Dill cleared his throat raspingly.

"Me? Oh, I had some uh my wages saved up. I used that." It never occurred to Billy that he had done anything out of the ordinary.

"*H-m-m!*" Dill cleared his throat again and rocked, his eyes on Billy's moody face. "I observe, William, that—er—they are not shipping any skates to—er—hell, yet!"

"Huh?" Billy had not been listening.

"I was saying, William, that I appreciate your fidelity to my interests, and—"

"Oh, that's all right," Billy cut in carelessly.

"—And I should like to have you with me on a new venture I have in mind. You probably have not heard of it here, but it is an assured fact that the railroad company are about to build a cut-off that will shut out Tower completely and put Hardup on the main line. In fact, they have actually started work at the other end, and though they are always very secretive about a thing like that, I happen to have a friend on the inside, so that my information is absolutely authentic. I have raised fifty thousand dollars among my good friends in Michigan, and

I intend to start a first-class general store here. I have already bargained for ten acres of land over there on the creek, where I feel sure the main part of the town will be situated. If you will come in with me we will form a partnership, equal shares. It is borrowed capital," he added hastily, "so that I am not giving you anything, William. You will take the same risk I take, and—"

"Sorry, Dilly, but I couldn't come through. Fine counter-jumper I'd make! Thank yuh all the same, Dilly."

"But there is the Bridger place. I shall keep that and go into thoroughbred stock—good, middle-weight horses, I think, that will find a ready sale among the settlers who are going to flock in here. You could take charge there and—"

"No, Dilly, I couldn't. I—I'm thinking uh drifting down into New Mexico. I—I want to see that country, bad."

Dill crossed his long legs the other way, let his hands drop loosely, and stared wistfully at Billy. "I really wish I could induce you to stay, William," he murmured.

"Well, yuh can't. I hope yuh come through better than yuh did with the Double-Crank—but I guess it'll be some considerable time before the towns and the gentle farmer (damn him!) are crowded to the wall by your damn' Progress." It was the first direct protest against changing conditions which Billy had so far put into words, and he looked sorry for having said so much. "Oh, here's your little blue book," he added, feeling it in his pocket. "I found it behind the trunk when everything else was packed."

"You saw—er—you saw Bridger, then? He is going to take his wife and Flora up North with him in the spring. It seems he has done well."

"I know—he told me."

Dill turned the leaves of the book slowly, and consciously refrained from looking at Billy. "They were about to leave when I was there. It is a shame. I am very sorry for Flora—she does not want to go. If—" He cleared his throat again and guiltily pretended to be reading a bit, here and there, and to be speaking casually. "If I were a marrying man, I am not sure but I should make love to Flora—h-m-m!—this 'Bachelor's Complaint' here—have you read it, William? It is very—here, for instance—'Nothing is to me more distasteful than the entire complacency and satisfaction which beam in the countenances of a new-married couple'—and so on. I feel tempted sometimes when I look at Flora—only she looks upon me as a—er—piece of furniture—the kind that sticks out in the way and you have to feel your way around it in the dark—awkward, but necessary. Poor girl, she cried in the most heartbroken way when I told her we would not be likely to see her again, and—I wonder what is the trouble between her and Walland? They used to be quite friendly, in a way, but she has not spoken to him, to my certain knowledge, since last spring. Whenever he came to the ranch she would go to her room and refuse to come out until he had left. H-m-m! Did she ever tell you, William?"

"No," snapped William huskily, smoking with his head bent and turned away.

"I know positively that she cut him dead, as they say, at the last Fourth-of-July dance. He asked her to dance, and she refused almost rudely and immediately got up and danced with that boy of Gunderson's—the one with the hair-lip. She could not have been taken with the hair-lipped fellow—at least, I should scarcely think so. Should you, William?"

This time William did not answer at all. Dill, watching his bent head tenderly, puckered his face into his peculiar smile.

"H-m-m! They stopped at the hotel to-night—Bridgers, I mean. Drove in after dark from the ranch. They mean to catch the noon train from Tower to-morrow, Bridger told me. It will be an immense benefit, William, when those big through-trains get to running through Hardup. There is some talk among the powers-that-be of making this a division point. It will develop the country wonderfully. I really feel tempted to cut down my investment in a store for the present, and buy more land. What do you think, William?"

"Oh, I dunno," said Billy in a let-me-alone kind of tone.

"Well, it's very late. Everybody who lays any claim to respectability should be in his bed," Dill remarked placidly. "You say you start at sunrise? H-m-m! You will have to call me so that I can go over to the hotel and get the money to refund what you used of your own. I left my cash in the hotel safe. But they will be stirring early—they will have to get the Bridgers off, you know."

It was Dill who lay and smiled quizzically into the dark and listened to the wide-awake breathing of the man beside him—breathing which betrayed deep emotion held rigidly in check so far as outward movement went. He fell asleep knowing well that the other was lying there wide-eyed and would probably stay so until day. He had had a hard day and had done many things, but what he had done last pleased him best.

Now this is a bald, unpolished record of the morning: Billy saw the dawn come, and rose in the perfect silence he had learned from years of sleeping in a tent with tired men, and of having to get up at all hours and take his turn at night-guarding; for tired, sleeping cowboys do not like to be disturbed unnecessarily, and so they one and all learn speedily the Golden Rule and how to apply it. That is why Dill, always a light sleeper, did not hear Billy go out.

Billy did not quite know what he was going to do, but habit bade him first feed and water his horse. After that—well, he did not know. Dill might not have things straight, or he might just be trying to jolly him up a little, or he might be a meddlesome old granny-gossip. What had looked dear and straight, say at three o'clock in the morning, was at day-dawn hazy with doubt. So he led Barney down to the creek behind the hotel, where in that primitive little place they watered their horses.

The sun was rising redly, and the hurrying ripples were all tipped with gold, and the sky above a bewildering, tumbled fabric of barbaric coloring. Would the sun rise like that in New Mexico? Billy wondered, and watched the coming of his last day here, where he had lived, had loved, had dreamed dreams and builded castles—and had seen the dreams change to bitterness, and the castles go toppling to ruins. He would like to stay with Dill, for he had grown fond of the lank, whimsical man who was like no one Billy had ever known. He would have stayed even in the face of the change that had come to the range-land—but he could not bear to see the familiar line of low hills which marked the Double-Crank and, farther down, the line-camp, and know that Flora was gone quite away from him into the North.

He caught himself back from brooding, and gave a pull at the halter by way of hinting to Barney that he need not drink the creek entirely dry—when suddenly he quivered and stood so still that he scarcely breathed.

"Oh, where have you been, Billy boy, Billy boy?

Oh, where have you been, charming Billy?"

Some one at the top of the creek-bank was singing it; some one with an exceedingly small, shaky little voice that was trying to be daring and mocking and indifferent, and that was none of these things—but only wistful and a bit pathetic.

Charming Billy, his face quite pale, turned his head cautiously as though he feared too abrupt a glance would drive her away, and looked at her standing there with her gray felt hat tilted against the sun, flipping her gloves nervously against her skirt. She was obviously trying to seem perfectly at ease, but her eyes were giving the lie to her manner.

Billy tried to smile, but instead his lips quivered and his eyes blinked.

"I have been to see my wife—"

he began to sing gamely, and stuck there, because something came up in his throat and squeezed his voice to a whisper. By main strength he pulled Barney away from the gold-tipped ripples, and came stumbling over the loose rocks.

She watched him warily, half-turned, ready to run away. "We—I—aren't you going to be nice and say good-by to me?"

He came on, staring at her and saying nothing.

"Well, if you still want to sulk—I wouldn't be as nasty as that, and—and hold a grudge the way you do—and I was going to be nice and forgiving; but if you don't care, and don't want—"

By this time he was close—quite close. "Yuh know I care! And yuh know I want—*you*. Oh, girlie, girlie!"

The colors had all left the sky, save blue and silver-gray, and the sun was a commonplace, dazzling ball of yellow. Charming Billy Boyle, his hat set back upon his head at a most eloquent angle, led Barney from the creek up to the stable. His eyes were alight and his brow was unwrinkled. His lips had quite lost their bitter lines, and once more had the humorous, care-free quirk at the corners.

He slammed the stable-door behind him and went off down the street, singing exultantly:

"—I have been to see my-wife,

She's the joy of my life—"

He jerked open the door of the shack, gave a whoop to raise the dead, and took Dill ungently by the shoulder.

"Come alive, yuh seven-foot Dill-pickle! What yuh want to lay here snoring for at this time uh day? Don't yuh know it's morning?"

Dill sat up and blinked, much like an owl in the sunshine. He puckered his face into a smile. "Aren't you rather uproarious—for so early in the day, William? I was under the impression that one usually grew hilarious—"

"Oh, there's other things besides whisky to make a man feel good," grinned Billy, his cheeks showing a tinge of red. "I'm in a hurry, Dilly. I've got to hit the trail immediate—and if it ain't too much trouble to let me have that money yuh spoke about—"

Dill got out of bed, eying him shrewdly. "Have you been gambling, William?"

Billy ran the green shade up from the window so energetically that it slipped from his fingers and buzzed noisily at file top. He craned his neck, trying to see the hotel. "Maybe yuh'd call it that—an old bachelor like you! Yuh see, Dilly, I've got business over in Tower. I've got to be there before noon, and I need—aw, thunder! How's a man going to get married when he's only got six dollars in his jeans?"

"I should say that would be scarcely feasible, William." Dill was smiling down at the lacing of his shoes. "We can soon remedy that, however. I'm—I'm very glad, William."

The cheeks of Charming Billy Boyle grew quite red. "And, by the way, Dilly," he said hurriedly, as if he shied at the subject of his love and his marriage, "I've changed my mind about going to New Mexico. I—we'll settle down on the Bridger place, if yuh still want me to. She says she'd rather stay here in this country."

Dill settled himself into his clothes, went over, and laid a hand awkwardly upon Billy's arm, "I am very glad, William," he said simply.

THE END.